D0438914

Geronimo Stilton

NO TIME to LOSE

THE FIFTH JOURNEY THROUGH TIME

Scholastic Inc.

Copyright © 2012 by Edizioni Piemme S.p.A., Palazzo Mondadori, Via Mondadori 1, 20090 Segrate, Italy. International Rights © Atlantyca S.p.A. English translation © 2018 by Atlantyca S.p.A.

The publisher does not have any control over and does not assume any responsibility for author or third-party websites or their content.

GERONIMO STILTON names, characters, and related indicia are copyright, trademark, and exclusive license of Atlantyca S.p.A. All rights reserved. The moral right of the author has been asserted. Based on an original idea by Elisabetta Dami. www.geronimostilton.com

Published by Scholastic Inc., *Publishers since 1920,* 557 Broadway, New York, NY 10012. SCHOLASTIC and associated logos are trademarks and/or registered trademarks of Scholastic Inc.

Stilton is the name of a famous English cheese. It is a registered trademark of the Stilton Cheese Makers' Association. For more information, go to www.stiltoncheese.com.

No part of this publication may be reproduced, stored in a retrieval system, or transmitted in any form or by any means, electronic, mechanical, photocopying, recording, or otherwise, without written permission of the copyright holder. For information regarding permission, please contact: Atlantyca S.p.A., Via Leopardi 8, 20123 Milan, Italy; e-mail foreignrights@atlantyca.it, www.atlantyca.com.

This book is a work of fiction. Names, characters, places, and incidents are either the product of the author's imagination or are used fictitiously, and any resemblance to actual persons, living or dead, business establishments, events, or locales is entirely coincidental.

Library of Congress Cataloging-in-Publication Data available

ISBN 978-1-338-21526-7

Text by Geronimo Stilton
Original title *Viaggio nel tempo-5*
Cover by Silvia Bigolin (pencils) and Christian Aliprandi (ink and color)
Illustrations by Danilo Barozzi, Silvia Bigolin, Carla De Bernardi, and Alessandro Muscillo (pencils), Christian Aliprandi (ink and color), and Piemme's Archives
Graphics by Marta Lorini and Chiara Cebraro

Special thanks to Andrea Schaffer
Translated by Shannon Decker
Interior design by Kay Petronio

10 9 8 7 6 5 4 3 2 1   18 19 20 21 22

Printed in China   38

First edition, February 2018

MY JOURNEYS THROUGH TIME

Dear Rodent Friends,
Welcome to my latest journey through time! My pal Professor Paws von Volt has taken us on some wild trips with his time-travel buddies.

THE MOUSE MOVER 3000

The Mouse Mover 3000 was the professor's first time machine. We used it to visit the dinosaurs, ancient Egypt, and medieval Europe ...

THE RODENT RELOCATOR

The Rodent Relocator was a more advanced machine. We used it to see Caesar's Rome, the Mayan cities, and the palace of Versailles during the time of the Sun King!

THE PAW PRO PORTAL

With the Paw Pro Portal, we reached the Ice Age, ancient Greece, and Renaissance Florence.

TAIL TRANSPORTER

We used the Tail Transporter to meet Cleopatra, Genghis Khan, Dante Alighieri, and Elizabeth I of England.

THE WHISKER WAFTER

This time we traveled on the Whisker Wafter, which can camouflage itself to fit into any era we travel through.

VOYAGERS ON THE FIFTH JOURNEY THROUGH TIME

Geronimo Stilton

My name is Stilton, Geronimo Stilton. I am the editor and publisher of *The Rodent's Gazette*, the most famouse newspaper on Mouse Island. I'm about to tell you the story of one of my most fabumouse adventures! But first, let me introduce the other mice in this story . . .

Thea Stilton

My sister, Thea, is athletic and brave! She's also a special correspondent for *The Rodent's Gazette*.

TRAP STILTON

My cousin Trap is a terrible prankster sometimes! His favorite hobby is playing jokes on me . . . but he's family, and I love him!

Benjamin Stilton

Benjamin is my favorite little nephew. He's a sweet and caring mouselet, and he makes me so proud!

Bugsy Wugsy

Bugsy Wugsy is Benjamin's best friend. She's a cheerful and lively rodent — sometimes too lively! But she's like family to us!

PROFESSOR PAWS VON VOLT

Professor von Volt is a genius inventor who has dedicated his life to making amazing new discoveries. His latest invention is the Whisker Watter, a new kind of time machine!

Robota

A new robot created by Professor von Volt, Robota is amazing — she can do any type of analysis! Her only defect is that she wants to be my girlfriend . . .

A SWEET SPRING MORNING . . . ALMOST!

One sweet SPRING morning in New Mouse City, I sat in my office rereading the article on the front page of my newspaper. The title read "Whale Emergency: Three New Species Beached!"

Moldy mozzarella!

Oh, excuse me, I forgot to introduce myself! My name is Stilton, *Geronimo Stilton*, and I'm the editor of *The Rodent's Gazette*, the most famous newspaper on Mouse Island!

Even though I was worried about the beached whales, it was a beautiful morning and I was in a fabumouse mood. I opened my office window and took a deep breath of fresh air. Ah, it smelled like *flowers*!

Suddenly, a **cloud of pollen** went up my snout. I exploded into a flurry of **sneezes**! I counted thirty-three in a row — **rats!** My snout began to **DRIP**, my face turned as red as the sauce on a double-cheese pizza, and both of my eyes swelled up like big balls of mozzarella!

Aaaaaaachoo!

Through my watery eyes, I saw a few pigeons come toward my

window. I thought they might want to land on my windowsill, since I always leave little PIECES of bread there for hungry birds. But too late, I realized that something wasn't right — the two pigeons flew strangely, almost as if they were lost. And before I knew what was happening, they flew straight into my head! SQUEAK!

What was going on?

I slammed the window shut and put a **bandage** over the bump forming on my head. I tried to go back to work, but I couldn't concentrate — I kept *sneezing*, my eyes watered, and my head hurt. I decided to call it a day and get some rest.

"Buh-bye, eberybody! I'b going hobe. I'b vewy sick!"*

It was only then that I realized that something was very wrong in the newsroom.

* I was trying to say, "Good-bye, everybody! I'm going home. I'm very sick!"

EVERYONE was sneezing endlessly, with **red snouts** and **swollen eyes** that looked like big balls of mozzarella!

Holey cheese, what was going on?

It was spring, not winter! The flu had already come and gone! Why was everyone **SICK** all of a sudden? I headed outside, muttering, "Hmmmm . . . first the sneezing, then the pigeons, then the epidemic in the newsroom. This is mousetastically STRANGE!"

As I walked home on tired paws, my belly started to rumble. I stopped at a cart to buy a triple-cheese *sandwich* and a large mozzarella **milkshake**, then sat down on a bench to eat. Oh, what a beautiful day — too bad I wasn't feeling good enough to really enjoy it!

Just then, I noticed a little **cloud** moving through the sky. But then it started to move faster and faster, and it was pointed right at me . . . no, at my *sandwich*!

That was no cloud — it was a flock of hungry **seagulls**, and they were attacking me! I tried to get

Blech!

away, waving my paws. I couldn't help noticing that the birds' feathers were slick with **oil**. Poor things! Though it was hard to feel too bad for them as they chased me down the street, **pecking** at my sandwich . . .

TOTAL GLOBAL EMERGENCY!

Right then, something in the pocket of my jacket began to vibrate.

Bzt! Bzzzt! Bzzzzzzzzzt!

It was my Voltophone! Alarmed, I pulled it out. If Professor von Volt was contacting me on that special phone, it meant that there was a serious **EMERGENCY**!

A **message** appeared on the screen: "*SECRET MEETING IN MY LABORATORY AT MIDNIGHT SHARP! ASK YOUR FAMILY FOR HELP!*"

Voltophone

This is Professor von Volt's secret phone, used exclusively for calling Geronimo during emergencies. It also has a radar and satellite navigation system.

Crusty cheese chunks, I didn't have any time to lose! I ran home and locked my doors and windows. Then I called Thea, Trap, Grandfather William, and Benjamin and asked them to meet at my house just before midnight.

That NIGHT, everyone arrived right on time — except Trap, of course. Benjamin's friend Bugsy Wugsy came along, too. I was about to tell everyone about Professor von Volt's mysterious MESSAGE when Trap finally showed up.

He burst into my mousehole without knocking. "Hey, everybody! Sorry I'm late, but I was busy inventing an incredible fascinating essence spray that will make me cheeseloads of money." He turned to me with a sly grin. "But I need a random rodent to test it on — like you, Geronimo! If my fascinating essence makes even you fascinating, Gerry Berry, who knows what effect it will have on normal mice, or those

who are already fabumousely *fascinating*, like me!"

Before I could squeak, he **spritzed** me with something that smelled like rotten cheese rinds and dirty socks! Cheese niblets! I was immediately surrounded by a swarm of **flies**.

I wasn't fascinating — I just stunk like a sewer rat!

I wanted to run and take a shower (or two or three) but I didn't have time! Grandfather William tapped his paws impatiently. "So, **GRANDSON**!

Why have you gathered us here in the middle of the night? This had better be important."

Thea **grumbled**, "I'm so tired I can feel my whiskers drooping."

I whispered, "Shhhh . . . this is a secret, an enormouse **secret**! Professor von Volt needs our help, but that's all I know so far. He's going to

give us DIRECTIONS so that we can meet him at his new secret laboratory."

Right on cue, the Voltophone *buzzed* and a message appeared: "*FOLLOW THE DIRECTIONS ON THE SATELLITE NAVIGATOR!*"

Without a moment to waste, we scampered out onto the streets of New Mouse City. The navigator

This is me!

This way!

took us on a long, winding route, to sidetrack any rodents who might be following us. Cheese and crackers, my paws were aching! Finally, we reached New Mouse City's main park. There, in the middle of a large field, the navigator screen showed a white *X*. How strange!

Holey cheese, had the navigator made a **MISTAKE**? The screen of the Voltophone lit up with the words, *"YOU HAVE ARRIVED AT YOUR DESTINATION."* But there was nothing around!

Suddenly, we heard a rumble, as if there were a large bee flying above us.

I looked up, but couldn't see a cheesecrumb, until . . .

ZAP! A transparent net closed around us and we were hoisted up into the air!

What a feline fright!

We began to fly through the air, hanging in the dark and holding on to our tails for dear life.

Great globs of Gouda, where were we headed? And who had mousenapped us?

After what seemed like hours, the 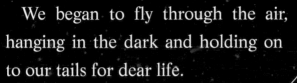 began to hoist us up higher and higher. We found ourselves being pulled inside the most **incredible** airship that I had ever seen.

And then I knew exactly where we were — this was Professor von Volt's new secret laboratory!

AN URGENT MISSION

As soon as we were safely inside the *airship*, Professor von Volt came to greet us. "I'm so glad you're here! Come in, we've been waiting for you!"

He led us into a **meeting room**. There, all the members of the von Volt family were seated around an **enormouse** crystal table.

I recognized some old friends: *Dewey von Volt*, Margo Bitmouse, Rusty Carr, Professor

The Incredible Airship

Here is Professor von Volt's new secret laboratory: an immense airship with many rooms and cabins. The ship has a control room, conference room, and testing laboratory, plus game rooms, a thermal bath, and a sauna!

Astrofur, Vivian von Volt, and **Roborat 8**. There was one scientist at the table who I didn't know. She was introduced as **Robota**, Roborat 8's cousin.

Professor von Volt invited us to sit at the table. "Thank you all for coming. I'm afraid we're facing a tremendmouse **emergency**: Mouse Island's environment is in grave danger! Maybe you have noticed more allergies among the rodents here lately? That's because the **AIR** is becoming more and more polluted and affecting our health!

Dewey von Volt

Margo Bitmouse

Rusty Carr

Professor Astrofur

Roborat 8

Robota

Vivian von Volt

Unfortunately, the **animals** are also suffering, because clean food and water are in short supply."

Hearing my friend's words, everything that had happened that day started to make sense.

HOLEY CHEESE!

Benjamin squeaked, "What can we do? I want to save the **environment**!"

"Mousetastic, Benjamin!" Professor von Volt said with a smile. "Each one of us can do a lot to help. If everyone on Mouse Island did his or her part, this would be a very different situation. But

Air Pollution

Have you ever heard of fine dust and carbon monoxide? These and other substances (given off by moving cars, heating plants, factory smokestacks, and many other things) change the quality of the air that we breathe, creating air pollution. This could be very damaging to our health — since polluted air can harm our noses, throats, airways, and lungs — as well as our planet.

now this is an EMERGENCY! So I've come up with a faster solution."

Thea looked curious. "Really? WHAT?"

Professor von Volt took a deep breath. "I want to send you to the past to meet the legendary *King Solomon*, a rodent famous for his great wisdom. Legend has it that he possesses a ring that can create harmony. We must ask to borrow it and bring it here, to New Mouse City, to restore balance to our environment. Then we'll return it to him in the past!"

Professor von Volt paused, then looked each of us square in the snout, one by one. "Do you want to leave on a new *journey through time*?"

My friends immediately squeaked, "Yesssssss!"

I seemed to be the only one who was a teeny, tiny bit uncertain. Oh, okay, I was **terrified**!

Grandfather William raised a paw. "I'm going to stay behind. After all, someone has to take care of

The Rodent's Gazette! With me in charge, maybe things will finally run **smoothly** again."

I **ROLLED** my eyes, then tried to stop my wobbling whiskers before squeaking, "Ahem, if I really must . . . I mean, if there isn't someone else . . . I guess I'll go."

Professor von Volt nodded solemnly. "Thanks to all of you — **especially** you, Geronimo. I know how difficult it is for you to leave. Please understand that the fate of our beloved island depends on this mission!"

Then he turned and gestured to Robota. "Now Robota will show you the **NEW TIME MACHINE**!"

Blah . . . blah . . . blah . . .

The bizarre little robot backed away from the table and began to project many blueprints and three-dimensional models into the air.

THE WHISKER WAFTER

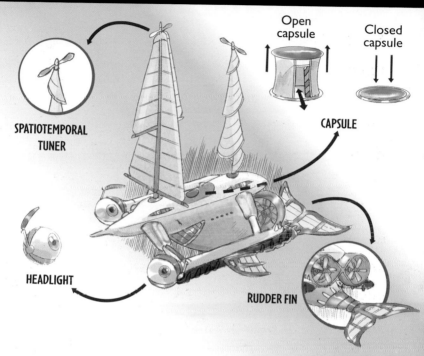

Open capsule

Closed capsule

CAPSULE

SPATIOTEMPORAL TUNER

HEADLIGHT

RUDDER FIN

AUTOMATIC DISTRIBUTORS OF TIME FUEL

The cubes of time fuel are kept here. Use the touch screen menu to choose which time period you would like to travel to, and the distributor will drop the right cube!

COMMAND CENTER

To operate the Whisker Wafter, the cube of time fuel is inserted here.

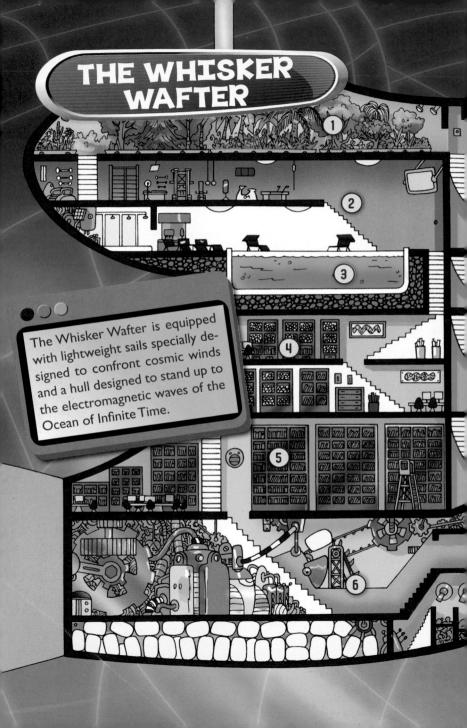

THE WHISKER WAFTER

The Whisker Wafter is equipped with lightweight sails specially designed to confront cosmic winds and a hull designed to stand up to the electromagnetic waves of the Ocean of Infinite Time.

"We call it the **Whisker Wafter**," she explained. "It is able to navigate the spatiotemporal waves and camouflage itself as a ship from different time periods to help you prevent detection."

The Whisker Wafter had all the comforts a mouse could hope for!

"How does it know which era to travel to?" Benjamin asked.

Professor von Volt grinned proudly. "Simple — it uses the memory of water molecules! The machine runs on time fuel, which is made of hydrogen and condensed into little **cubes**. The time fuel cubes each contain frozen water, and each one will take you to a different era. To make the time fuel cubes, we needed samples of water from different eras, so we extracted ancient layers of ice from Slippery Slopes Glacier."

"How will we communicate on our

travels? Won't they speak different languages?" asked Bugsy Wugsy.

"Ah, yes!" responded Margo. "It's complicated science, but before landing, the Whisker Wafter will **transmit** the necessary language directly to the travelers' brains!"

Squeak — a transmission directly to my brain? How **FUR-RAISING**!

I wanted to ask a cheeseload more questions, but Professor von Volt cut me short. "Let's get going — there's no time to waste! **Robota** will travel with you. She can help with any questions that come up during the journey. Are you ready for takeoff? **Good luck!**"

He pressed a button with his paw. The hatches opened, and our seats **PLUMMETED INTO DARKNESS**! Holey cheeeeeeeeeeese!

I'm in Charge Here!

After a tail-twisting free fall, we found ourselves on the deck of the Whisker Wafter. Luckily, our chairs were equipped with rocket brakes, so we all had a soft, smooth landing!

Robota led us into the Control Room and hollered, "Here's how it is done! You find the right cube of time fuel from the era you want to travel to, insert it into the right container, and press the green button. Is that clear? Don't worry — since I know that you are simplemice, I will be next to the captain. Speaking of which, who is going to be in charge?"

Trap squeaked, "Me! I'm in charge!"

He got a cube of time fuel from the distributor and inserted it into the container. He hit the green button before anyone could stop him.

DESTINATION . . .

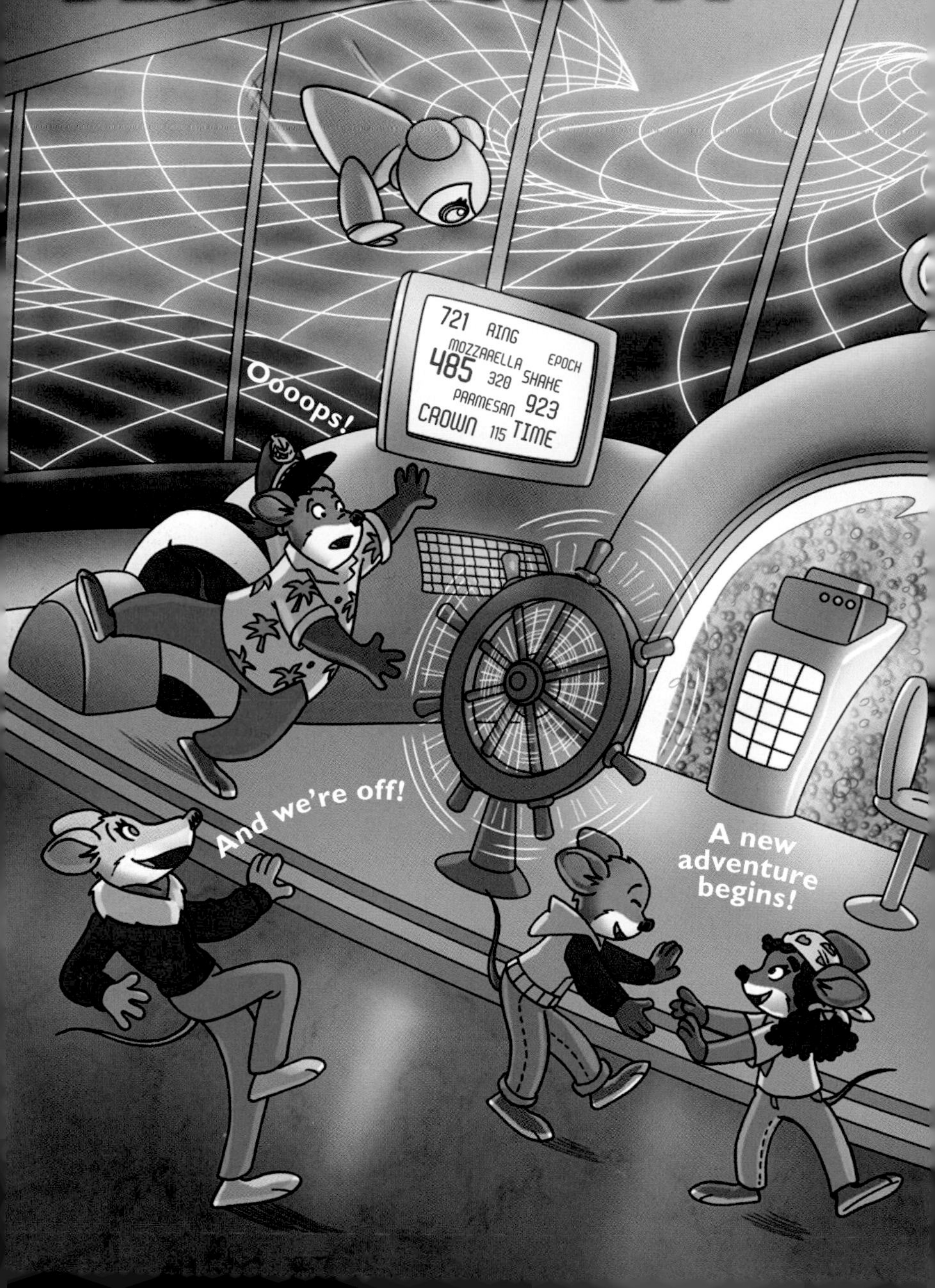

"Trap where did you send us?" I squeaked.

The Whisker Wafter began to vibrate, there was a *FLASH OF WHITE LIGHT*, and we found ourselves riding the electromagnetic waves of the Ocean of Infinite Time.

We were officially off on our latest *journey through time*!

To keep us busy during the trip, Robota showed us around the rest of the Whisker Wafter, screeching, "Here is the thermal bath, and here is a gym. Next door, you will find a room of **COSTUMES**, with clothes from all different historical eras . . ."

I'm not sure what she said after that, because I couldn't finish the tour. My poor stomach began to dance UP and down, down and UP. I felt like I was going to toss my cheese!

NAPOLEON'S
COURT

WHO ARE YOU SQUEAKING ABOUT?

After a trip that seemed never-ending, the Whisker Wafter finally came to a stop. We were enveloped in a bright FLASH OF LIGHT — we had arrived!

What a nightmarish trip! My stomach was twisted in knots, and my fur turned greener than moldy mozzarella. Lucky me — it turns out I suffer from time sickness!

Have you ever heard of it? Time sickness is more annoying than car sickness, more obnoxious than dizziness, more queasy than seasickness, more terrible than a toothache, and more painful than a stomachache! I've suffered from all of those, but time sickness is by far the worst of the **worst** of the **worst**!

I tried to think pawsitively. After all, our journey would be over soon! Our task on this trip was **very simple** — we just had to find the legendary King Solomon, ask to borrow his ring, return to New Mouse City with it, and then send the ring back to the past. Compared to our previous journeys through time, this was going to be **EASY CHEESY**! (I didn't know then just how **WRONG** I was . . .)

I went up to the deck to take a look outside and immediately realized that something wasn't right. The Whisker Wafter was **MOORED** along the banks of a large river, next to a group of tall palaces. We were definitely not in the era of King Solomon! So where were we?

The first **rays** of dawn sparkled on the surface

of the river. I looked around and noticed that the Whisker Wafter had transformed into an elegant merchant **SHIP**, transporting a load of **super-stinky** cheese. Whew — that smelled like a boatload of good cheese gone **bad**!

On the pier, I could see a few rodents unloading all sorts of merchandise from their boats: spices,

What a stink — yuck!

Florentine tapestries, lace, Brazilian **cocoa**, and Dutch tulip **bulbs**.

The wide streets lining the river were decorated with **GARLANDS** of laurel and white **roses**. At the center of the garlands was a large golden **N**. That reminded me of something . . . but what?

I was admiring the scene when a rodent with

Hey, lazy rat!

long **SiDEBURNS** called to me from the shore. "Hurry, Hurry! I'm talking to you, lazy rat! Why aren't you unloading the ship? He is arriving today! It's finally the big day!"

Luckily, the Whisker Wafter had directly translated his language for me — this rodent was squeaking in **FRENCH**! We were in France! The clothes and hairstyles I could see made it very clear: we had traveled back to the **1800s CE**! But who was this rodent that was supposedly arriving today?

I was more mixed up than a mozzarella milkshake!

I cleared my throat and called down to the mouse. "Excuse me! Can I ask you a question? Who are you squeaking about, and why is today a big day?"

The mouse proudly showed me a tricolor *rosette* with a gold capital *N* in the middle.

Then he burst into laughter. "Ha, ha, ha! You look like a cheesebrain, but you're actually a pretty funny mouse, monsieur! Everyone knows that today is the coronation ceremony to officially crown the great *Napoleon Bonaparte* emperor of France!"

Suddenly, he caught a whiff of the super-stinky cheese in the hold of the Whisker Wafter and added, "Cheesy creampuffs! That's the authentic cheese course, seasoned to perfection — just how Napoleon likes it. I'd recognize that unmistakable **aroma** anywhere!"

He waved a paw in front of his snout and added, "**HURRY!** Unload it, and bring it to the palace kitchens immediately. Napoleon will have a lady with him — and she only wants to smell **roses** when she passes through here!"

A MINOR MISTAKE

I wanted to ask what lady he was squeaking about, but I had more important things to get my tail in a twist over — like the fact that we'd traveled to the **WRONG** time period!

We had to leave as **soon** as possible!

I quickly waved good-bye to the rodent and **RAN** down belowdecks.

I spotted Trap and exclaimed, "We've landed in Paris, on the day of the coronation of Napoleon Bonaparte: December 2, 1804! We're nowhere near the era of King Solomon!"

Trap waved a paw. "You're squeaking about a **MINOR MISTAKE**! Napoleon, Solomon, they both end in 'on.' And they're both mice with lots of power, wealth, and jewels . . . and probably rings, too!"

Robota **shot** Trap a look, as flashes of

electric-blue light sizzled all around her. Then she EXPLODED, "A minor mistake?! It's your fault that we were off by twenty-seven centuries, which is twenty-seven hundred years — I'll save you the count in minutes and seconds! **Foolish rodent!** Total cheesebrain! **YOU** chose the cube of time fuel! **YOU** brought us here! *This is all your fault!*"

I held up my paws and tried to make peace. "Don't fight! We need to get out of here, and that's that. We have to finish our MISSION, so let's leave right away and —"

Robota interrupted me, batting her eyes. "Impossible, cheddarcheeks! We can't leave right away. The Whisker Wafter must cool down for at least three hours before going on a new journey. Otherwise, it runs the risk of **DISINTEGRATING** — and taking us with it!"

Cheddarcheeks!

I twisted my tail into a knot. "Did you say disintegrate? Rats! I'm too fond of my fur!"

Trap rubbed his belly and grinned. "Fabumouse! This means that we can stay for Napoleon's coronation. I'd bet my whiskers that there will be a banquet! Yum — I love French FOOD. They say it's the best in the world . . ."

Just then, Thea, Bugsy Wugsy, and Benjamin entered the control room. Bugsy Wugsy jumped on my back and squeaked at top volume, "Uncle G! We're heeeere!"

I tried to stay calm. "Yes, we're here, just not where we meant to be! But let's take a **LOOK** around. Maybe we can even help with Napoleon's coronation. What do you say?"

Thea's eyes lit up. **"Holy Swiss cheese!** If Napoleon is here, **SHE** will be, too!"

"Who?" I asked.

"**Joséphine**, the empress! One of the most fascinating rodents of all time!" Thea exclaimed. "I've always dreamed of meeting her. There are so many things I'd like to ask her . . ."

I clapped my paws for attention. "Okay, let's get ready! We need to dress in Empire style.* We'll pretend that we're a **merchant family** from Corsica with a shipment of extra-stinky cheese for Napoleon!"

Thea sniffed the air. "We can pretend to be merchants, but the super-stinky cheese seems very real! **Putrid Parmesan, what a disgusting smell!"**

---

* This is one term for the style of clothing worn during the Napoleonic era. To learn more, go to page 44–45!

As we headed for the costume room, Robota said, "Professor von Volt told you that the Whisker Wafter would be **CAMOUFLAGED** to fit into whatever time period we traveled to, right? I'm afraid if we were any more camouflaged than this, we'd be **DEAD**!"

Trap **laughed**. "Definitely, we'd die from the stench!"

Robota didn't answer, because she was already giving Thea and Bugsy Wugsy instructions on how to **DRESS** like fancy ladies of the era.

Trap and I ended up wearing jackets with long tails, vests, and funny tight pants. There was also a wig for me, but I refused to put it on. It was full of authentic fleas from the 1800s! **YUCK!**

Finally, Robota miraculously miniaturized herself, transforming into a **brooch** and pinning herself to my tie. "Isn't it wonderful, sweet Geronimo? I'll be close to you! You can read me all your travel notes, and I can keep you company!"

For the love of cheese, there was no way out of this one. Robota had me pinned!

EMPIRE STYLE

During the Napoleonic age, the popular fashion was known as the Empire style. This manner of dress was inspired by the clothing of the ancient Greeks and Romans.

FEMININE FASHION

French women of the early 1800s wore clothes that were reminiscent of Greek and Roman statues — ankle-length dresses with high waists that fluttered with every step. The dresses often had short, billowy sleeves, and the ladies used shawls to shelter themselves from the cold.

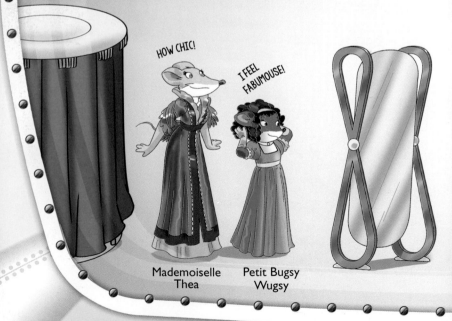

Mademoiselle
Thea

Petit Bugsy
Wugsy

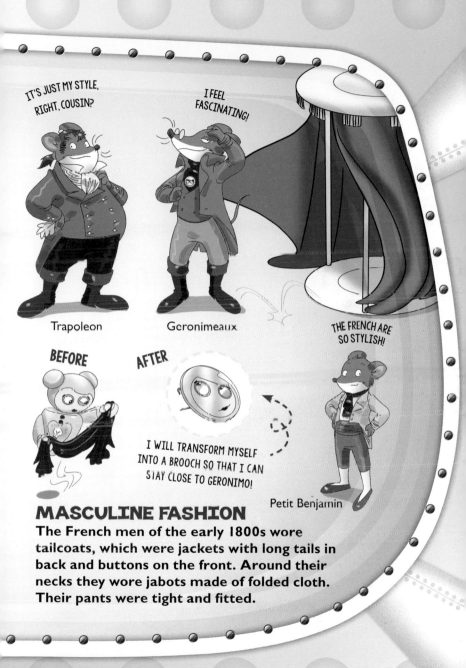

IT'S JUST MY STYLE, RIGHT, COUSIN?

I FEEL FASCINATING!

Trapoleon

Geronimeaux

THE FRENCH ARE SO STYLISH!

BEFORE

AFTER

I WILL TRANSFORM MYSELF INTO A BROOCH SO THAT I CAN STAY CLOSE TO GERONIMO!

Petit Benjamin

MASCULINE FASHION

The French men of the early 1800s wore tailcoats, which were jackets with long tails in back and buttons on the front. Around their necks they wore jabots made of folded cloth. Their pants were tight and fitted.

IT'S REALLY, TRULY HER!

I had just finished putting the finishing touches on my outfit when I heard a voice **SQUEAK** from the pier. "Hey, you on the boat! Didn't I tell you to hurry up with that cheese? The imperial court is arriving! If you don't hurry . . . **Snip**! He might **cut** off your tail!"

How stinky!

We hurried to unload the stinky **cheese** from the Whisker Wafter's hold . . . but it was too late! We could already hear the **TRUMPETS** announcing the arrival of the court.

Suddenly, the **NOISE** of a thousand cannons slashed through the silence, saluting the passage of the emperor and the empress.

Startled, I **stumbled** and fell into the Seine,* taking the wheels of extra-stinky cheese with me!

RATS!

BADABOOOM!

BOOOOOM!

BOOM!

Ooooops!

What's happening?

Aaaaaaaah!

* The Seine is the river that runs down the center of Paris.

Luckily, everyone was too busy to notice. All around, mice were squeaking, "It's him, it's really him! The emperor!"

"And she's here, too! It's really, truly her — the empress!"

"*Long live Napoleon!*"
"*Long live Joséphine!*"
"*Long live France!*"

I reemerged from the chilly river, gasping and sputtering. Once I caught my breath, I chimed in, "Long live the emperor! Long live the empress!"

As I splashed and flailed in the **water** of the Seine, the imperial carriage passed right by our ship! For a second, I thought I spotted a **KIND FACE** looking out at us from the window of the golden carriage. Could that really be the empress, looking at me — a **SOAKING-WET** rodent floundering in the river? Holey Swiss cheese!

I thought I must be wrong, but a white-gloved paw gestured and the imperial carriage stopped.

"Rotten rat's teeth!" I squeaked. "Is the emperor going to slice off my tail?"

I could picture it already: the imperial guards would cuff me, and . . . snip!

Instead, two valets hurried to open the carriage door, two others rolled out a red CARPET on the pavement, and two more mice scattered white rose PETALS. Finally, a paw covered with a silk slipper stepped out of the carriage.

No one dared to squeak. It was really her — the empress!

In a calm voice, she said, "Rescue that mouse and bring him to me!"

My heart began to **POUND**. A mouse as tall as a refrigerator fished me out with a hook, lifted me by the tail, and dropped me at the feet of Joséphine. Cheesy creampuffs, how mortifying!

I bowed and stammered, "Your M-majesty, f-forgive me if I disturbed your *imperial* court, I mean, your *imperial* parade, I mean, if I slowed your *imperial* coronation . . . but, I beg you, don't cut off my tail!"

She was silent.

EVERYONE was silent.

I could hear my own knees shaking with fear. CLACK, CLACK! CLACK, CLACK!

I even heard the sound of the drops of water falling from my clothes and whiskers. Drip! Drip! Drip!

The empress suddenly burst into *laughter*.

"Ha, ha, ha! What in the world are you squeaking about? What a funny mouse! I stopped to help you, not to **cut** off your tail! Now tell me, how did you end up in the river?"

I couldn't believe my fabumouse luck . . . but I also felt like a total cheesebrain! "Forgive me, Your Highness! I knew that you or your husband would never cut off my tail! Your beauty just confused me and caused me to make a complete fool out of myself!"

I made a fool out of myself!

Huh?

She **SMILED**. "You are forgiven, monsieur. What is your name, and where are you from?"

I bowed and said, "My name is *Geronimeaux Stiltoneaux*, and I am a cheese merchant. I came from Corsica with my family to present your imperial husband with his favorite **CHEESE**! We were preparing to unload and transport the cheese to the imperial palace when the **CANONS** startled me. The cheese and I both ended up in the water."

I fell to my knees in front of her. "I beg you, Your Highness, forgive my total, complete, enormouse blunder!" Then I picked a rose from a nearby shrub and pawed it to her. "My cheese and my pen are at your service, Your Imperial Highness!"

At that moment, *Napoleon Bonaparte* himself descended from the carriage!

He walked over and studied me with icy

eyes. Then he grabbed my **ear** and squeezed it enthusiastically. "I like this mouse! You are sincere, GENEROUS, and **Gallant**! Maybe a little too gallant . . . careful not to be too gallant with my Joséphine! Or else — **SNiP**!"

Squeak!

You're a nice mouse!

IMPERIAL EAR PULLING
Napoleon's personal butler, Louis Constant Wairy, told tales about his master pulling the ears of friends, acquaintances, and even his personal doctor, whenever he liked someone and was in a good mood!

AN IMPERIAL PINCH

I felt like I was about to faint with fear, but Napoleon gave me another imperial pinch on the ear. **Youch!** That will wake a mouse up!

He laughed. *"Mon amie,** I was joking! I wouldn't really cut off your tail — at least not right now, ha! But be careful, I am a VERY JEALOUS rodent. Joséphine is the most beautiful mouse I've ever seen, and we're a perfect match, since I am the most handsome, most famouse, and most powerful mouse in the **WORLD**!"

He clapped his paws and ordered his servants, "Make sure that Monsieur Geronimeaux is dressed in warm, dry clothes. He and his family will be my guests today at the CORONATION and banquet!"

---

* In French this means "my friend."

Before he left, he said, *"Au revoir, mon amie!"* When we see each other again, I will officially be the emperor. In the meantime, I will think about what to do with you — I have a feeling you could be useful, and I never misjudge a mouse! I think you could become my taster . . . or maybe my advisor . . . or my librarian . . . or my official biographer . . . we'll see!"

Then he got back in the carriage, and the court headed for the Notre Dame Cathedral, where the coronation *ceremony* would take place.

Great globs of Gouda, we were going to witness a mousetastically **IMPORTANT** historical event! My WHiSKeRS trembled, and I might have fainted if Robota hadn't given me a tremendmouse shock, shrieking in my ear, "Geeeeeronimooo! I saw the way you looked at that Joséphine!"

I rolled my eyes just as Thea,

Grrrr . . .

* In French this means "Good-bye, my friend."

Bugsy Wugsy, Benjamin, and Trap joined me in the carriage that had been prepared for us.

Thea tugged at her whiskers. "Look at this **MESS** you got us into, Geronimo! Who knows when we'll be able to leave? Our mission is very urgent, you know — we have to HURRY!"

I sighed. "I promise you that we'll try to scamper away as soon as possible. But for now, let's **learn** as much as we can from this experience. After all, it's not every day you get to help with the coronation of an emperor!"

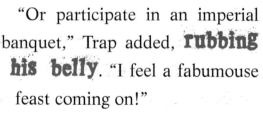

Mmmm!

"Or participate in an imperial banquet," Trap added, **rubbing his belly**. "I feel a fabumouse feast coming on!"

I held up my paws. "For the love of cheese, try not to embarrass me, Trap! Behave yourself — don't eat with your paws, don't wipe your mouth on the shirt of the mouse next to you, and **no burps**! If we stick one paw out of line . . . **SNIP**! They'll cut off our tails!"

As we rolled toward the cathedral, Robota wouldn't stop chattering at me. "Geronimo, don't be impressed by that Joséphine, she's nothing special . . ."

Benjamin squeaked, "She seems pretty special to me. She's about to become the EMPRESS, after all!"

Bugsy Wugsy added, "Plus she's nice — and mouserifically beautiful, too."

Robota began to **cry** oily robot tears. Oh, cheese and crackers, how ridiculous!

Finally, we reached our destination. I couldn't believe it — the *ceremony* was about to begin, and we were going to witness it firstpaw!

THE CORONATION OF NAPOLEON

The coronation took place on December 2, 1804, with a lavish ceremony in the Notre Dame Cathedral in Paris. Napoleon placed the French emperor's crown on his own head and the empress's crown on the head of his wife, Joséphine de Beauharnais. It was the first time in the history of France that a sovereign crowned himself!

The Golden Bees

The golden bees, the oldest symbol of the kings of France, were embroidered with golden thread on the red velvet capes that Napoleon and Joséphine wore for the coronation.

The Two Crowns

During the ceremony, Napoleon wore two crowns. One, made of golden laurel leaves, was reminiscent of the crowns that the ancient Romans put on the heads of victorious generals. The other was a more traditional crown of French kings.

What a mouserific event!

I couldn't help feeling moved when Napoleon placed the crown on Joséphine's head. Thea and Bugsy Wugsy wouldn't stop talking about the **fabumouse** gowns worn by Napoleon's sister and the lady mice of the court.

Robota gave me a lot of interesting **information** about Napoleon.

ZAP!

Don't be too impressed with Joséphine! Did you know that when she was a girl . . . blah, blah . . . blah, blah . . .

Napoleon

First Name: Napoleon
Last Name: Bonaparte
Born: in Ajaccio, Corsica, on August 15, 1769
Famous Quotes:
"Imagination rules the world."
"The word *impossible* is not in my dictionary."
"He who hazards nothing, gains nothing."

His Life:
As a celebrated official in the French army, Napoleon became head of state as first consul in 1799, and emperor in 1804. He was able to greatly expand the French Empire, but his successes ended with a tremendous defeat during the French invasion of Russia. He was exiled in 1814 and later abdicated his powers. Napoleon died on May 5, 1821.

PARBLEU, THIS IS AN EPIDEMIC!

As soon as the ceremony ended, I thought we might be able to sneak away, return to the Whisker Wafter, and continue our **MISSION**. Taking advantage of the general confusion, we **CREPT** quietly through the crowd toward the exit.

Where do you think you're going?

Squeak!

Suddenly, a paw grabbed my shoulder and a **loud voice** boomed, "Hey, where do you think you're going? The emperor invited you to be his guest! His every desire is an order, understand? If you don't understand, I will make you understand, or my name isn't **CAPTAIN PARBLEU**!"

The mouse that had spoken was many heads taller than me, with a coat covered in gleaming **MEDALS**. Rats — this was one of Napoleon's official guards!

I frantically tried to find an excuse for leaving. "I . . . well . . . I didn't want . . . but . . . to tell you the truth . . . I mean . . . in reality . . ."

Luckily, Thea came to my aid. My sister always knows what to do when I have my tail in a twist! She winked at me, then crumpled to the ground. "Ooooooooooh, I think I might faint! I need some air . . ."

I'm going to faint!

Captain Parbleu hurried to help her. I looked at him sheepishly. "Well, as you can see, **my sister** isn't feeling well. I was taking her outside for a little air, even though we didn't want to leave."

The captain was **HORRIFIED**. Great balls of mozzarella, Thea was a fabumouse actress!

I'm going to faint!

Seeing the effect Thea was having, **Bugsy Wugsy** decided to jump in, too. She muttered, "I don't feel well, either . . . I need some **AIR** . . ."

Unfortunately, she forgot to wink at me — so I didn't realize she was pretending! I **DOVE** to catch her, but lost my B A L A N C e and smacked my head on the pavement.

I **fainted** — for real! The last thing I heard was the guards exclaiming, "It's an **EPIDEMIC**! Everyone is fainting!"

BONK! BAM!

I fainted!

Nothing's Wrong
with Me!

When I finally opened my eyes, I rubbed my head. *"Ouch, what a bump!"*

I looked around. I was lying in a canopy bed, covered with silk that had been embroidered with gold bees and white roses. The delicate smell of **roses** filled the room. Holey cheese, where was I?

Before I had time to figure it out, the door flung open and Thea, Bugsy Wugsy, Benjamin, and Trap rushed in.

I was mousetastically **happy** to see them!

I didn't even have time to hug them before the door opened again. Four rodents with **STRANGE** objects in their paws walked in. Could they be gifts from the emperor? **Fabumouse!**

Unfortunately, I was very, very wrong — those

weren't gifts! The mice were **DOCTORS**, and they were carrying instruments for the remedies of the time . . . which were very, very unpleasant. My fur stood on end when I realized that they had brought them for me!

I jumped to my paws and squeaked, "I'm just fine! I'm all healed, nothing's wrong with meeeeee!" Then I tried to scamper away, but the doctors were determined to cure me at all costs. Even as they tried to restrain me, they fought among themselves.

"It's clear that he needs some medical **attention**!"

He needs some medical attention!

I have just the thing!

This would be ideal!

Let's inspect his ears!

"Oh no, don't you see how agitated he is? I have just the thing!"

"You don't know what you're doing!"

I took advantage of the confusion to ESCAPE, with my family right on my tail. I climbed through the window — **LUCKILY** we were on the ground floor! — and found myself in the garden. But I landed right on a holly bush and my **undertail** was suddenly full of thorns! **SQUEEEEEAK!**

While I jumped and howled with pain, I noticed someone approaching out of the corner of my eye. **Cheese niblets** – it was the empress!

Huh?

Ha, ha, ha!

Hee, hee!

Escape, Uncle!

I have an urgent appointment!

THE LIFE OF AN EMPRESS IS HARD!

The empress SMILED. *"Cher Monsieur** Geronimeaux, I see that you are feeling better. You slept for a long time! Lucky you — I was busy with parties, BANQUETS, official conversations, balls, fireworks. What an imperial bore!" She sighed.

She paused, then said melodramatically, "Oh, the life of an empress is **hard**!"

You're so funny!

The empress went on. "I came here to Château de Malmaison to relax with my beloved roses and get away from the crowds."

Squeak!

* In French this means "dear sir."

Joséphine

First Name: Joséphine
Last Name: de Beauharnais
Born: in Les Trois-Îlets, on the island of Martinique on June 23, 1763
Distinguishing Characteristics: Extremely charming
Her Secret: A passion for plants, especially roses! The Souvenir de la Malmaison rose is named after her rose garden.

Her Life:
Joséphine spent her childhood in Martinique, until 1779, at the age of sixteen, when she went to Paris to marry Alexander de Beauharnais. She had two sons with him, Eugene and Hortense. She was widowed and then met Napoleon. They fell deeply in love and married in 1796. Their marriage ended in 1810, and Joséphine died in 1814.

As she told us about her different commitments as an empress, I couldn't help admitting that she was right — her life did seem awfully stressful!

"Oh, enough complaining!" she said suddenly. "Tonight, you are all invited to the banquet!"

She turned to Thea and Bugsy Wugsy. "You, my dears, will be my ladies of honor. And

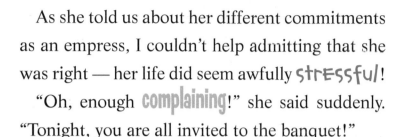

you, Trapoleon, will be the Imperial Mouster of Ceremonies!" Looking at Benjamin and Bugsy Wugsy, she said, "You seem to be lively little mouselets! You can be in charge of Fortuné..."

When he heard his name, a tiny dog ran up — and **bit** my leg! Then he leaped into Benjamin's arms and licked his face.

Joséphine looked at me, her eyes sparkling. "Rest now, my dear Geronimeaux! The **emperor** would love for you to become his personal librarian, so he may put you to work soon. Just be careful — our previous librarian didn't last very long!"

Before anyone could squeak, she smiled at each of us in turn. "Best wishes, fair rodents! Enjoy my home!"

I wanted to ask her why the previous librarian hadn't lasted very long — being a librarian isn't a dangerous job, after all! — but I didn't dare. Instead, I bowed and said, "Thank you. My family and I are honored to be your guests here!"

Joséphine gave a little shrug. "You should see the château in the spring . . . which reminds me: before I go, I want to show you a little secret!"

She led us over to a large iron-and-GLASS building. "Here is where I keep my most marvemouse treasures! Go ahead and have a look around. I need to go change for the banquet — I've already

been wearing this same dress for six hours!"

We entered the building — it was a greenhouse! I was squeakless. Mousetastic, exotic plants and at least 250 DIFFERENT SPECIES of roses were growing inside!

As we wandered through the beautiful flowers, we heard pawsteps approaching. Holey cheese — it was Napoleon himself! He pinched my ear and exclaimed, "I've been looking everywhere for you, Geronimeaux! CONGRATULATIONS, I just appointed you my librarian. Isn't that fabumouse? I hope that you'll last longer than the last mouse — he was gone in less than a week!"

I was dying to ask what had happened to the previous librarian, but Napoleon went on. "What do you think of my beautiful Joséphine's greenhouse? There's so much more of the palace to see. Follow me!"

Neptune Pool

Joséphine wanted to create this pool of water alongside a statue of Neptune, the Roman god of sea and water, for the romantic atmosphere. She even imported rare black swans from Australia to swim there!

Summer Pavilion

Napoleon had this building furnished like a studio. This is where he often did his work during the summer!

Greenhouse

More than 250 species of roses and numerous exotic and tropical plants were cultivated in the large, heated greenhouse.

Malmaison

Temple of Love
This building resembles the temples of the ancient Romans.

The Château de Malmaison, an elegant residence with a large park, just outside of Paris, was purchased by Joséphine in 1799, while Napoleon was busy in the conquest of Egypt and the Near East. It was their primary residence between 1800 and 1802. Here, they hosted state meetings, receptions, balls, performances, and social events. In 1802, the couple moved to the Palace of the Tuileries in Paris, but the Malmaison was always special to Joséphine. She chose to retire there after she and Napoleon divorced, dedicating herself to caring for her beloved plants.

CONGRATULATIONS, GERONIMEAUX!

Escorted by a small group of **dignitaries** and **SOLDIERS** of the guard, Napoleon led us around the palace — from the stables to the attics, from the ballroom to the smallest storage closet!

While we walked, Napoleon asked me to jot down all of his thoughts.

I tried to protest, kindly telling him that my paws hurt and that I was not his personal secretary or scribe. "**CONGRATULATIONS, GERONIMEAUX!**" he squeaked. "I have just promoted you to be my personal secretary and scribe! Now take **notes** as I dictate a few sentences. One day my words will be famouse!"

All of the soldiers of the guard responded in unison, "Oui, mon général!"*

It was becoming clear that all of the soldiers of the guard, all of the servants, and all of the royal advisors always did their best to agree with Napoleon.

"**MON GÉNÉRAL**, you are right!"

"Whatever you say, **MON GÉNÉRAL**, is the truth!"

"**MON GÉNÉRAL**, you are the greatest, the best, the most mousetastic leader in the world!"

I frantically took notes on an enormouse scroll, trying not to tip over the **ink** as I scribbled!

Thundering cattails, what an awful job!

To make matters worse, it seemed like all of Napoleon's servants were glaring at me and whispering as I walked by: "Pssst . . . pssst

*In French this means "Yes, my general!"

. . . pssst . . ."

"Who does that mouse think he is?"

"He just got here, and he's already Napoleon's favorite!"

One of Napoleon's advisors, who had very long blond SIDEBURNS and icy-cold EYES, gave me a wicked look as he stuck out a paw to TRIP me. Then he muttered, "Oh, excuse me — I didn't see you!"

Hee, hee, hee!

Oooops!

Crusty cat litter, I was sure that he had tripped me on purpose!

I **stumbled** and ended up snoutdown on the ground. The ink spilled on my head . . . and **all over** my precious notes! Rats!

For a second, I feared that Napoleon would **cut off** my tail for being a horrible klutz.

Instead, he pinched my ear and pulled me to my paws, laughing. "You're quite the **JOKER**, Geronimeaux! Congratulations — you have just been promoted to COURT JESTER!"

The rodent who had tripped me **HISSED** in my ear, "For now, he seems to prefer you. Don't get too **FULL** of yourself, rat — it won't last long, and neither will you! I, Duke Louis Rodente de Gruyère von Brie, am and will always be Napoleon's **favorite**. Understand?"

Then he walked ahead of me with great strides, gnawing on a mint CANDY. It seemed like he had something very important to take care of.

I shivered. Swiss cheese on rye, I had officially made an **enemy**!

The emperor was surrounded by jealous rodents with a hunger for power!

But I didn't have time to think too much about it, because Napoleon began to ask me for advice on military STRATEGY. Rotten rat's teeth!

"Tell me, Geronimeaux, what do you think of the British?" he mused. "And the *AUSTRIANS*? In your opinion, can I trust the Prussians? And what would you think of a nice military campaign in Russia?"

Silence fell on the group. Everyone looked at me, awaiting my response.

My whiskers trembled and I twisted my tail into knots!

What could I say? And what would happen if Napoleon didn't like my answer? Would he cut off my tail? SNIP!

I tried stalling. "Your Majesty, I am nothing but a poor cheese merchant —"

But Napoleon interrupted, patting me on the back and booming, "Congratulations, Geronimeaux! I just promoted you to be my advisor! What do you say?"

No, Thanks, I'm Allergic to Cannons!

I was tempted to tell him the truth, even at the cost of having my tail CUT OFF!

Instead, I tried to remember how things went for Napoleon during his **MILITARY CAMPAIGNS**. Great balls of mozzarella, that's right — the Russian campaign was a disaster!

I squeaked up. "Your Majesty, I don't know anything about ALLIANCES, but you might want to stay away from Russia, and especially Waterloo!"

Napoleon stared at me, shocked. "How dare you? Why must I **give up** Russia? And Waterloo? I have never given up on anything in my LIFE!"

Everyone whispered, "That **cheesebrain** popped out of nowhere — how could he squeak to the emperor like that?"

Jena
1806

Leipzig
1813

Svezia

Friedland
1807

Borodino
1812

United Kingdom of
Great Britain and
Ireland

Kingdom of
Norway and
Denmark

Kingdom
of Prussia

Russian
Empire

Waterloo
1815

Grand Duchy
of Warsaw

Smolensk
1812

Napoleonic Empire

Confederation
of the Rhine

Austrian
Empire

Swiss
Confederation

Kingdom
of Italy

Illyrian
Provinces

Austerlitz
1805

Kingdom of
Portugal

Kingdom
of Spain

Kingdom
of Sardinia

Kingdom
of Naples

Ottoman Empire

Kingdom
of Sicily

NAPOLEONIC EMPIRE
in 1812

- ■ Territory of the Napoleonic Empire
- ■ Allies or Dependent States
- ■ Enemies of Napoleon
- ⚑ Battles Won
- ✗ Battles Lost

Thanks to his alliances and military victories, Napoleon was able to create a vast empire. By 1812, at the height of his power, he controlled almost all of Europe! But when Great Britain (a bitter enemy of France) made an alliance with Russia, Sweden, Prussia, and Austria, things became more difficult for Napoleon. The disastrous campaign of Russia (1812), followed by defeat in Leipzig (1813) and Waterloo (1815) signaled the collapse of the Napoleonic Empire.

Duke von Brie, who had just entered the room, joined the others and insisted, "No one is ever allowed to contradict you, Your Majesty!"

I was sure that Napoleon was going to have my tail cut off, but I had to squeak the truth. "Your Majesty, the choice is yours, but if I were you I would not leave for Russia. You risk being defeated by General Winter!"*

Napoleon put a paw on my shoulder and said admiringly, "Geronimeaux, you really are a COURAGEOUS mouse!"

Duke von Brie's snout turned red with rage, but I sighed in relief. Maybe my tail was safe, after all!

The emperor looked me up and down, from the ends of my whiskers to the tip of my tail, then grunted, "I like courageous mice — I think I'll

---

* According to history, this expression indicates that the Napoleonic troops were not defeated by armed enemies during the Russian campaign, since they technically won the battles, but were hugely decimated by the cold weather and related hardships.

promote you to GENERAL!"

Putrid cheese puffs, what?

Without thinking, I exclaimed, "I would be the librarian, the personal secretary, the scribe, the court jester, and the advisor . . . If you want, I can also become the taster, stable boy, or the officer who shines all of your imperial boots, but I can never, ever become a general! I am a **PEACEFUL** mouse. I don't want to know anything about war, battles, combat, or skirmishes. I am allergic to cannons, bullets, and GUNPOWDER!"

I nominate you general!

No, thanks! I am allergic to cannons!

When I stopped talking, everyone was silent. No one dared to squeak. I waited for Napoleon to get angrier than a cat in a cage and order my tail to be cut off — SNIP! Luckily, at that moment, the beautiful empress entered the room, accompanied by her **maids** and smelling of roses. At the sight of Joséphine, Napoleon forgot everything . . . he even forgot to be angry with me!

Right then, all he could see was Joséphine!

I was also squeakless — what *elegant* and *graceful* mice! I shook my snout and realized that two of the empress's maids were staring at me. One actually *smiled* at me and **WINKED**! Slimy Swiss balls, I couldn't believe it!

It was only when one of the maids made a **silly face** at me that I recognized them.

Thundering cattails, it was Bugsy Wugsy and Thea! Benjamin stood nearby, dressed as a page

What grace!

What splendor!

boy holding the little dog *FORTUNÉ* in his paws. When he saw Napoleon, the little dog leaped out of Benjamin's paws and tried to bite the emperor's calf. Holey cheese! Benjamin hurried to **grab** him, and Napoleon said, "Good job, young mouselet! I don't know why, but that dog has something against me . . ."

He ordered that a **BONE** be brought out on a silver platter, and the little dog chewed on it happily. Whew!

Napoleon offered his arm to Joséphine, and everyone headed for the **BANQUET** hall together. We were all led by Trap, acting as the Mouster of Ceremonies of the Court!

Unfortunately, when I walked past my cousin, he gave me another **SPRITZ** of his *fascinating essence.* Rancid ricotta! It took effect immediately — all of the ladies began **fighting** over who would stand next to me!

I turned positively pink with embarrassment. Trap, on the other paw, grinned, rubbing his paws together. "Good, good . . . my *fascinating essence* works! If **even** Geronimo becomes irresistible, who knows what effect it will have on mice who are already fascinating, like me!"

This mouse is mine!

Heeeelp!

I'll marry him!

Paws off, he's mine!

PSSST! PSSST! PSSSSST!

The maids all began squeaking, "That mouse is mine!"

"He's mine!"

"PAWS OFF, I saw him first!"

"No way, I'm his favorite!"

Just then, Joséphine came over to me, took my paw, and said, "My dears, enough fighting, I beg you! I will extend my arm to Geronimeaux. You don't mind, do you, dearest Napoleon?"

All of the ladies took a step back, bowing. Then they began to whisper among themselves.

"Pssst . . . pssst . . . did you see that?"

"Joséphine and that Geronimeaux!"

"Pssst . . . won't the emperor be jealous?"

Napoleon shot me a look that made me shiver.

Then he said to Joséphine, "If you really must, dear, go ahead with Geronimeaux. But I don't know how you can be accompanied by any less than the most fascinating, most **brilliant**, most HANDSOME rodent in the world — me!"

In that moment, Duke von Bric stepped forward. He rudely bumped me out of the way, then boomed, "Your Majesty, don't trust this mouse!"

Quick as lightning, he reached into my jacket pocket and pulled out a fine linen PAWKERCHIEF.

Oops!

Your Majesty, don't trust him!

Hmmm . . .

The pawkerchief smelled like **roses**. How had it gotten there? I had never seen it before!

Napoleon took it in his paws. "This is the pawkerchief that I gave to Joséphine! It even smells like roses — I would recognize Joséphine's perfume anywhere!"

I tried to defend myself. "Your Ma-ma-ma-majesty, I have ne-ne-ne-never seen that pawkerchief before. Rodent's honor!"

"Not another word. **Search that traitor rat!**" he ordered.

Two enormouse soldiers grabbed me by the

Aaagh!

paws and turned me upside down. Two sparkling earrings fell out of my pockets.

Holey cheese, how did they get there? I had never seen them before in my life!

Napoleon picked them up. Turning GREEN with jealousy, he said, "Joséphine, my beloved, these are the earrings that I gave you for your birthday. Why does this Rat have them?"

"I don't know, dear Napoleon," Joséphine said, confused. "He must have stolen them! Though he doesn't seem like the kind of mouse who steals JEWELS from others . . ."

Robota whispered, "See? I told you to not trust that Joséphine!"

I didn't have time to respond, because Napoleon thundered, "ARREST this rat and his whole family! Tomorrow morning at dawn, cut off all their tails — Snip! Snip! Snip!"

I squeaked at the top of my lungs, "Nooooo, not

my family! Cut off my tail if you must, but they have nothing to do with it!"

Napoleon stood pawsitively still for a moment. Finally, he said, "You are **COURAGEOUS**, mouse. So be it! I will cut off only **YOUR** tail, tomorrow at dawn."

Luckily, Thea had a flash of brilliance. I can always count on my sister! She ran up to Napoleon, a TEAR sliding down her face, and squeaked,

Sob, sniff . . .

Tomorrow, snip!

"Your Majesty! You are the most *gallant* mouse in the world! The most fascinating! The most courageous! The most iNTeLLi8eNT!"

Thea watched as Napoleon nodded smugly, and then she continued. "You can demonstrate that you are also the most *merciful*, the most RIGHTEOUS, and the most GENEROUS in the world. Give my poor brother a chance to prove his innocence!"

Napoleon walked **BACK** and **FORTH** across the room for what seemed like a lifetime, paws clasped behind his back and a dark look on his snout. Finally, he exclaimed, "So be it, rat! Prove your innocence, or I will have your tail *cut* off. If you can't convince me, then tomorrow morning at dawn — **SNIP**! And no fooling around; Parbleu, my most loyal guard, will keep an **EYE** on you!"

Password: Melted Cheese!

Napoleon clapped his paws and **Parbleu** scampered in. He was the same enormouse guard that we had met at the coronation! From that moment on, he was like my SHADOW. He didn't leave me alone for a minute — not even when I had to go to the bathroom! Crusty cat litter, how annoying!

Before we parted, Napoleon reminded me, "Remember, you have until **DAWN**. Then . . . SNIP!"

As soon as he'd left, I burst into tears. "Oh, we're going to be stuck here forever — and, to make it even worse, I'll be tailless!"

Thea, who is the coolest and calmest mouse I know, cut in. "Don't get your tail in knots! It's time for a family meeting in my room — immediately!"

We gathered in her room as fast as our paws would carry us, and began discussing what to do.

Parbleu stayed on guard outside the door, sharpening his sword: Ziiiip! Ziiiip! Ziiiip!

While he sharpened, he hollered, "Go ahead

and talk, I have plenty to keep me busy — I'm making sure my **sword** will be ready for tomorrow, when I cut off Geronimeaux's tail!"

While my WHiSKeRS wobbled, I tried to analyze exactly what had happened with Joséphine's pawkerchief and earrings. There had to be a way to prove my innocence!

Thea frowned thoughtfully. "Geronimo, are you SURE that you didn't see anyone who could have put these in your POCKETS?"

"No, he was probably too distracted by beautiful Joséphine," Bugsy Wugsy teased.

I put a paw over my heart. "Cross my heart, I wasn't! Rodent's honor!"

Robota batted her metal eyes. "Of course he wasn't distracted by her. Who could possibly win over that enormouse heart of yours? Maybe a pretty little ROBot? Me, for example? When should we have the wedding, dearest Geronimo?"

I threw my paws in the air. "Cut it out, Robota! There's no time for your SILLINESS!"

Who could win that enormouse heart of yours?

"Quit your squeaking!" Thea said. "Let's focus and come up with a PLAN.

We're running out of time. What RAT could have put the empress's pawkerchief and earrings in your pocket?"

I shrugged. "I got the impression that many mice were JEALOUS of the attention Napoleon was giving me — lots of them WHiSPeReD when I walked by! But maybe I'm wrong. There's something else that's been bothering me, too: Joséphine told me that the previous **librarian** 'didn't last long.' What did she mean?"

"I'm sure he was fired, or left, or . . . **died prematurely**, Cousin!" Trap said, wiggling his eyebrows at me.

Thea was all business. "Okay, so there are TWO THINGS that we need to investigate — who might be jealous of Geronimo, and the premature disappearance of the librarian! Slimy Swiss balls, I wonder if those two things could be CONNECTED . . ."

"There's something else to think about," I added. "Who could have had access to Joséphine's JEWELS? There can't be very many rodents who could enter her PRIVATE quarters and get their paws on her precious jewelry!"

Thea clapped her paws in excitement. "Fabumouse thinking, Geronimo! Now there's no time to waste, so let's shake a tail and start INVESTIGATING. We'll split up; meet back here in six hours. The password will be

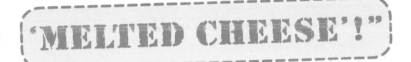

'MELTED CHEESE'!"

HERE'S HOW WE DIVIDED UP

QUESTION #1: Who had access to the empress's rooms and jewels? Thea planned to investigate this by chatting with Joséphine's mice-in-waiting.

QUESTION #2: Who wanted to frame Geronimeaux? Benjamin and Bugsy Wugsy would sneak around the palace, quietly eavesdropping on conversations among members of Napoleon's entourage.

THE INVESTIGATION:

QUESTION #3: Did the real thief leave any pawprints?

Robota and I would analyze the evidence — the pawkerchief and earrings — in search of microscopic traces of the real culprit.

QUESTION #4: What happened to the previous librarian?

Trap, as Mouster of Ceremonies of the Court, decided to chat with the servers, to find out who the librarian was and why he disappeared.

WHEN DO WE GET ENGAGED?

Everyone else left the room as **FAST** as their paws would carry them, while I stayed behind with Robota to **examine** the evidence. We had to look carefully for any microscopic **traces** left by the real thief!

Outside the door, **Parbleu** continued sharpening his sword. The sound made my fur stand on end — if we didn't figure this out by the next morning, they were going to **CUT OFF** my tail! We locked the door so Parbleu couldn't pop in to see what we were doing. Then Robota returned to her normal size and got to work! She was a HiGHLY aDVaNCeD robot, so she could analyze the evidence using the most modern techniques. Thundering cattails, for once I was **GLAD** to have her around!

But not for long.

While Robota worked, she chattered on and on . . . **AND ON**. "Oh, what would you do without me? Admit it — you'd be lost! So when do we get **engaged**? Soon, I hope. I would love a spring wedding."

Squeak!

Yank!

I tugged on my whiskers, trying to keep my cool. "Let's focus on finding clues!"

While I was lost in thought, she suddenly reached over and plucked one of my WHiSKeRS. Rancid ricotta, that hurt!

I had barely recovered from the shock when her **mechanical arm** reached over again — and plucked a hair off my tail with some tweezers!

"What in the name of all things cheesy are you doing?" I squeaked.

"Oh, calm down!" she said. "I only plucked a few samples for an analysis of your **DNA**, cheddarcheeks. I thought I'd compare your DNA with the DNA of the **THIEF** who tried to set you up."

She placed the whisker and the hair inside a flask and began to **vibrate** like a washing machine. After a few seconds, she spit out a sheet of paper containing an enormously long series of numbers and letters: it was the **SEQUENCE** of my DNA!

DNA

DNA is a type of "identity card" in humans and almost all other organisms. It is an acid that is most often found in the nucleus of cells, and contains all the genetic information of each individual or organism. It is arranged as two long strands twisted together to form a double helix spiral. Geronimo's was made of cheese!

Geronimo's **DNA** is extra cheesy!

Let's see . . .

Robota took the earrings and the pawkerchief and observed them with a **superextramoustronica lens**. It could enlarge things up to a mousilion* times!

It was truly marvemouse!

She tried **different** enlargements and made many **ANALYSES**.

Rat-munching robots, I had never seen her concentrate so hard!

Finally, she sighed. "I'm sorry, dearest, there's nothing else I can do. I found traces of rose **PeRfume** and one of Joséphine's **hairs** on the earrings.

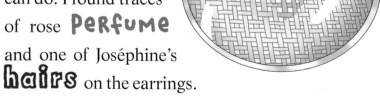

---

* Mousilion: a mouse unit of measurement.

The pawkerchief just had some drool from her little dog and traces of a super-concentrated essence of mint, sage, eucalyptus, and honey. That's it!"

Chattering cheddar, that combination was very familiar. It reminded me of someone — **BUT WHO**?

I tried and tried, but I couldn't remember! Maybe I was too stressed to think clearly, or maybe I was distracted by the sound of saber-sharpening outside. **SQUEAK!**

Just then, someone knocked at the door.

"**Password!**" I cried.

"Is it 'moldy mozzarella'?" Trap responded uncertainly.

"Wrong!" Robota replied. "You can't come in!"

My cousin tried again. "Jumping Jack cheese? Frozen fondue? Slimy Swiss balls? Creamy cheese sauce?"

Trap went on and on for ten minutes, until I was ready to tear out my whiskers. "Enough! Robota, let him in! Time is ticking, and my **TAIL** is on the line!"

"Thanks, Geronimo," Trap said. "What is the password, anyway?"

Only Trap could list **750** different types of cheese in ten minutes but forget a password as simple as . . . as . . . as . . .

Rat-munching rattlesnakes, I'd forgotten it, too!

Robota rolled her eyes. "What a couple of cheesebrains! We'll be lucky to solve this case with investigators as forgetful as you two! The password is 'melted cheese'!"

MIGHTY MOZZARELLA STICKS!

"So, what did you find out?" I asked, turning my attention,to Trap.

He rubbed his stomach and burped. "I found out that French **COOKS** are the best in the world! *Yum, what a meal!*"

"And what else?" I asked.

"That's it!" Trap said simply.

Burp!

Ooh, he was really toasting my cheese! "Mighty mozzarella sticks, Trap, my tail is on the line and all you can think about is **eating**?!"

He waved a paw and added, "Oh, I forgot! I also found out about a secret recipe for mint candies to cover up bad breath.

When we get back to New Mouse City, it's going to make me money paw over fist! The sister of the cousin of the aunt of the sister-in-law of Napoleon's **butler** told me that Duke von Brie has her prepare it for him personally. She found a super-concentrated essence of mint, sage, eucalyptus, and honey that seems to be the only combination that will cover his stinky breath. He pops those candies nonstop!"

I jumped to my paws and squeaked, "A super-concentrated essence of mint, sage, eucalyptus, and honey? Are you sure? Maybe we've found the culprit after all: Duke von Brie! There are traces of a super-concentrated essence of mint, sage, eucalyptus, and honey on Joséphine's pawkerchief!"

I paused for a moment, thinking. "Before we accuse him, we need more proof. Duke von Brie could have left a trace of the candy on the pawkerchief when he took it and showed it to Napoleon."

At that moment, Bugsy Wugsy, Benjamin, and Thea burst through the door!

Bugsy Wugsy grinned. "Uncle G, we went all around the palace and kept our ears wide open!"

Benjamin nodded. "We discovered that there's a ghost in the basement of the palace! For the past few days, no one has wanted to go down there because you can hear bangs, screams, and the sound of chains rattling."

I turned as white as a slab of mozzarella.

Trying to keep my whiskers from wobbling, I said, "That's strange, since ghosts aren't real! We need to go take a look."

"Afterward, we tried to go into Joséphine's room, but it was locked," Bugsy Wugsy continued. "But we met the *maid* who had just finished cleaning the room, and we got our paws on the **trash**.

Here — maybe there's some interesting evidence in here."

I had to admit, those mouselets were full of smart ideas! I pinched my snout and began pawing through the **stinky** trash.

Among the dust, crumpled paper, and leftover food scraps, I also found a mint candy, sticky and covered with dust.

HOLEY CHEESE!

Maybe Duke von Brie really *did* go into Joséphine's room!

Strange!

It stinks!

Blech!

At that point, Thea squeaked up. "I found out that there's only one rodent who has access to the empress's JEWELS: Mademoiselle Fondue, the first maid of the court, who happens to be engaged to . . . take a guess!"

Everyone responded in unison, "Duke von Brie!"

Rancid ricotta, everything was becoming clear! The last thing we needed to do was meet the ghost that was living in the basement. But we had to hurry — time was running out! I grabbed the oil lamp, and together we scampered down into the BASEMENT of the palace (followed by Parbleu, of course).

As we headed down the stairs, we heard the clanking of chains and eerie howls. How fur-raising! What could it be — a terrifying monster or a hungry WERECAT? Squeak!

Finally, we arrived in front of a little door.

The **ghost**, or monster, or whatever it was, was surely right beyond the door. Cheese and crackers, my fur was standing on end!

I was about to faint with fear, but Parbleu bravely stepped forward with his sword and gave the door a **shove**. "I'll go first. Hey, monster, it's just you and me! I'm not **scared** of anything!"

The door

opened with a crash: **BANG!**

We all held our breath.

But there wasn't a monster inside the TINY room — there was just an **elderly** rodent, tied up and gagged!

SORRY YOU HAVE TO LOSE YOUR TAIL!

Parbleu exclaimed, "Cheesy creampuffs — you're PIERRE, the old librarian! You're not dead after all! But what are you doing here?"

Thea took the GAG off the poor rodent, who said, "I'm not dead yet, but if you hadn't found me, I don't know what would have happened. Von Brie LOCKED me in here and threw away the key!"

I couldn't help getting my tail in a twist. "What a SeWeR Rat! Why would he do something so slimy?"

Pierre sighed. "A few days ago, I was walking in the garden and I accidentally overheard him squeaking with Mademoiselle Fondue, his fiancée. He asked her to help him steal the empress's jewels. She wanted nothing to do with it, but he told her that if she didn't help, it meant that she didn't love him! Suddenly, I sneezed. Von Brie realized I was there — and that I had overheard everything. Before I could hightail it away, he **tied me up** and IMPRISONED me down here!"

"And now that rat is trying to blame me for STEALING the jewels!" I cried. "But he won't get away with it — not if we have anything to **SQUEAK** about it!"

Thea, Trap, Bugsy Wugsy, and Benjamin all hugged me. "Your tail is safe!"

Parbleu **held up** a paw. "Wait just a second! Whether or not Geronimeaux's tail will be cut off is up to Napoleon! You are mousetastic rodents, but it's not up to me to decide. I follow my general's ORDERS!"

With that, he tied us up tightly and led us away. "It's **DAWN**! Time to present yourselves to Napoleon. No more stories, no whining, and above all, no **FAINTING** — I'm talking to you, Geronimeaux! Act strong and respectful, or I'll cut off **all** of your tails!"

Poking my UNDERTAIL with his super-sharp sword — youch! — he led us to where Napoleon, Joséphine, and the court were waiting.

Even though Pierre was **mouserifically exhausted**, he came along to testify on my behalf. Napoleon welcomed us with a frown and

scrutinized each of us one by one. Cheese and crackers, even my fur was quivering!

All of the ladies sighed and began to sniffle. "Poor Geronimeaux!"

"He was so fascinating!"

"It's such a shame they're going to cut off his tail!"

Even though my whiskers trembled with fear and my legs were as soft as cottage cheese, I tried to act confident.

"Your Imperial Majesty," I said, "I'm ready to prove that I am not the thief."

KEY

EARRINGS

CANDY

Napoleon looked at me in surprise. I continued, "One: as you know, the only person who has the key to your imperial wife's room is the First Maid of the Court, Mademoiselle Fondue, who is engaged to Duke von Brie.

Two: whoever entered the empress's room to steal her earrings used a key. The door showed no signs of being broken into. Three: the thief dropped this mint candy on the ground, then threw it away." I held the candy up in my paw. "We found it in the trash being taking out of the room."

Out of the corner of my eye, I saw Duke von Brie turn as pale as a slab of mozzarella.

I pointed a paw at the rat and squeaked, "That's the culprit right there, Duke von Brie — he's famouse for his mint *candies*!"

Von Brie was squeakless for a moment. Then he hollered, "How dare you! Anyone could have left that candy to **FRAME** me — maybe even you!"

"But your mints also **stained** the pawkerchief!" I said. I turned to Napoleon. "You can see it with this special lens I invented. I'd bet all the cheese in Paris that there are mint stains

on the empress's jewelry box key, too."

After thinking for a moment, Napoleon ordered, "Mademoiselle Fondue, show us the key to the jewelry box!"

The First Maid of the Court stepped forward, trembling. She bowed to Napoleon, pulled the key from a CHAIN that was hanging around her neck, and placed it in his paw.

Napoleon examined it for a bit, and then

squeaked, *"It's true!* I can see green stains even without the lens! And this key smells like mint, eucalyptus, sage, and honey. I have a fabumousely acute sense of *sight* and SMELL, you know!"

He turned to Duke von Brie and thundered, "Well, Duke, tell me — what are your **FAMOUSE** candies made of?"

Von Brie tried to invent something on the spot, but Trap fanned the recipe under his snout. "Ooh, I know! Your candies are made of mint, sage, eucalyptus, and honey. And they're prepared especially for **you**!"

Duke von Brie was about to protest again, when Pierre the `librarian` stepped forward. He had been standing just outside the door, listening.

Napoleon was flabbergasted when he saw the librarian. "Pierre! You aren't **dead**!"

"Mon général, I am here as a witness for

Geronimeaux," Pierre said quietly. "A few days ago, I overheard Duke von Brie plotting to steal the empress's jewels. He caught me and **TIED ME UP** in the basement of the palace. But Geronimeaux saved me — rodent's honor!"

Napoleon got to his paws, thundering, "Duke von Brie is guilty of **high treason**! I will have his tail cut off!"

But the duke had disappeared! **RATS**!

Mademoiselle Fondue dropped to her knees and burst into tears. "Forgive me, Your Majesty! I let my fiancé convince me to go along with a **terrible crime**!"

Joséphine held up a paw. "You made a mistake, but I can see that you are genuinely sorry. I will forgive you — this time."

Napoleon turned to me. "Geronimeaux, of course I won't CUT OFF your tail now. But how can we ever repay you?"

"Your Majesty, I only want to take my family back home," I said. "There are mousetastically urgent affairs awaiting us."

He **SMiLeD**. "Absolutely — you can leave! But first, come closer . . ."

Holey cheese, what now?

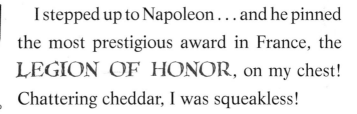

I stepped up to Napoleon . . . and he pinned the most prestigious award in France, the LEGION OF HONOR, on my chest! Chattering cheddar, I was squeakless!

Then he put a paw on my shoulder and said, "I'm sorry you're leaving — you were an **excellent** librarian, advisor, and court jester, but above all, you are a loyal and sincere mouse! *Congratulations, Geronimeaux!*"

A fancy carriage with the imperial coat of arms was called to take us back to the Whisker Wafter. Finally, it was time to continue on our **journey**!

We walked aboard and headed belowdecks. Trap ran ahead and raced toward the **control room**. Rancid ricotta! Who knew where he was going to send us this time?

We had to **stop** him — our tails depended on it!

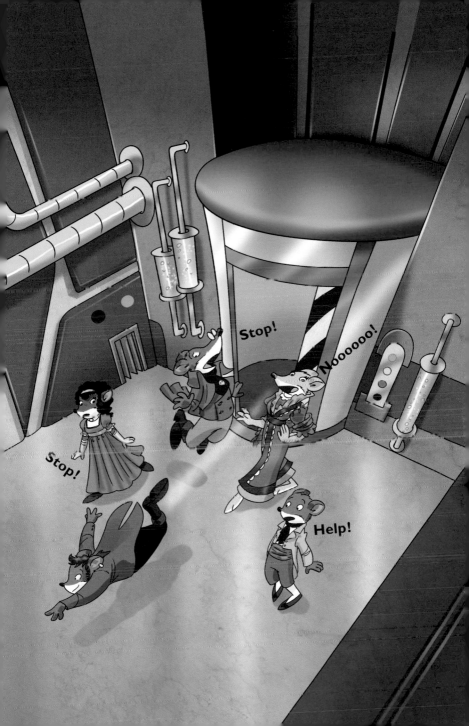

GLOOORB! GLUUURB! GLAAARB!

Trap ran to the time fuel *DISTRIBUTOR* as quickly as he could. He grabbed a random cube and put it into the special container before anyone could stop him.

"That should do it!" he squeaked.

I ran so fast trying to stop him that I tripped —

and hit my head on the floor! **THWACK!**

Before I could even process what had happened, the Whisker Wafter began to vibrate. There was a flash of light, and suddenly we were cruising along on the **WAVES** of space and time!

Lucky me, I began to feel sick almost immediately. To make matters worse, Robota fawned over me with a fan, and Thea and Trap began **FIGHTING**.

"Trap, you have to tell us what you put in there!"

"Oh, who could say . . . I chose it in a **HURRY**!" Trap scoffed. "I think . . . approximately . . . roughly . . . oh, who can remember? I know I can't! Anyway, I am the **CAPTAIN**, and therefore I am always right. I am never wrong."

They went on fighting like that for what felt like hours!

In the meantime, the Whisker Wafter **ROCKED** and I tossed my cheese. Ugh!

After what seemed like an eternity, there was finally another *FLASH OF LIGHT*.

We had arrived . . . but **WHERE**?

I crawled up on deck and took a quick look around. This time I had a pretty good idea of where we were, because I could see an enormouse DRAGON'S HEAD right under my snout! We were on a Viking ship!

THE AGE
OF THE
VIKINGS

A MENACING SHIP

This wasn't a real dragon's head, of course — otherwise, I wouldn't be here to tell you about this adventure! No, it was a WOODEN dragon's head decorating the Whisker Wafter, which had transformed into a longship.*

We had landed in the age of the VIKINGS! To make things even more exciting, we were right in the middle of a big storm. Yikes — this was no good for a 'fraidy mouse like me!

It was all paws on deck, as we desperately tried to keep the ship from crashing. I grabbed one oar to use as a rudder, but it snapped in half. We were at the mercy of the waves!

Squeeeeeak! I was so scared out of my fur that I forgot to be seasick!

Luckily, the sea finally calmed down

---

* A longship is a typical Viking boat, long and narrow with a shallow hull.

before the ship was horribly damaged. We ran aground on a **BEACH**, in the middle of a fjord surrounded by steep, high cliffs.

"We're safe!" I exclaimed, flopping to the ground.

"Maybe," Robota said.

"Huh?" I asked, sitting up. "What do you mean?"

Robota shrugged. "Well, the Vikings were **tough**!"

"Er . . . how tough?" I asked, trying to keep my voice from quivering.

"Marvemousely **tough**!" she said. "They were great navigators, famouse for not being afraid of anything. Some of them were fierce raiders."

"Fierce raiders?" I squeaked.

"Yes, cheddarcheeks, are your ears filled with cheese?" Robota went on. "But don't worry, many of them were peaceful traders. Anyway, my little

THE VIKINGS

The Vikings were a population of great navigators and courageous warriors. Originally from Scandinavia, they lived between approximately 800 and 1100 CE. The Vikings traveled a lot, but their arrival often evoked terror because they were known for their raids! They also loved to wrestle in order to stay in shape. As experienced sailors, it is said that they may have reached North America five hundred years before Columbus.

LONGSHIP

BOW

HULL

The classic Viking longship had a long hull and was not very deep. Because of this, the Vikings could sail their boats right up to beaches without running aground — to the surprise of their enemies!

When sailing in enemy seas, the Vikings sailed on boats that had menacing, carved wooden heads on the bows.

VIKING FASHION

While we don't know exactly what the Vikings wore, we do know that they preferred comfort over elegance. Their clothes and shoes were fairly simple, and brooches and pins were the most popular accessories. The Vikings used them to fasten their clothes, since they didn't have buttons or zippers!

THE FEMININE STYLE

The Viking women wore long dresses with slightly shorter tunics on top. These were fastened with two pins, often connected by a chain. The women used this chain instead of pockets, to hang things that they wanted to carry with them!

WHAT DO YOU THINK OF MY BRAIDS?

WHAT A BEAUTIFUL TUNIC!

Bugsorik

Thella

I FEEL TOUGH!

Geronimord

THIS JACKET IS COMFORTABLE!

Trappolund

HOW FUNNY!

Beniamik

THE MASCULINE STYLE

Viking men wore wool pants and a tunic that was tightened at the waist with a large belt. To protect themselves from the cold, they often wore warm hats and cloaks latched with a brooch, and sometimes wool leg wraps.

cheesepuff, don't even think about escaping just yet — you know that the Whisker Wafter needs to cool down!"

She was right. We might as well have a look around, since we were stuck! We all ran to the COSTUME room to find the right clothes.

As I got dressed, I muttered, "I hope we only meet the peaceful Vikings today . . ."

Suddenly, someone on the beach yelled, "Ahoy, you in the ship! Come out, or we'll use an ax to force you out!"

Ahoy!

Great Gouda globs, these didn't seem like peaceful types! I peered out and saw a group of Vikings, solid as **cliffs**, strong as ROCKS, and as dangerous as a stormy Sea. My whiskers began to wobble. Our tails were on the line again!

Unfazed, Trap jumped down from the boat, swinging his **SWORD** above his head, and landed right in front of the largest Viking in the bunch. He patted the Viking on the shoulder and said, "Ahoy, Big Belly! I am Trappolund,

Hmpf!

Hmpf!

Hmpf!

and I am the captain of this ship. That 'fraidy mouse back there — see his snout peeking out? — is my cousin *Geronimord*."

It looked like the enormouse Viking was about to make micemeat out of Trap with one strike of his ax. Holey cheese, I had to do something!

I tried to leap down from the longship, but I slipped and banged my head on the side of the boat, biting my tongue! Dazed, I got to my paws, stumbled to the beach, and slipped on a pile

Help!

Eek!

Ouch!

of wet **algae**. I did a somersault with a **twist** and landed on my feet, right between Trap and the enormouse Viking!

I gathered my **COURAGE** and yelled, "Yop, errybody! Don't hurt my couthin!" (I meant to say, "Stop, everybody! Don't hurt my cousin!" but my tongue was swollen!) The Viking thundered, "Oh, I like these mice! You are **lacking** strength, but you seem fabumousely **COURAGEOUS**! Where arc you from?"

Squeak!

Yop, errybody!

FESTIVAL OF THE TOUGH VIKING!

Thea, Bugsy Wugsy, and Benjamin joined us. "Hi, you massive mouse," Thea said with a smile. "My name is Thella, and this is Benjamik and Bugsorik. We just arrived from the far reaches of Mousijland, a wonderful place rich in forests, FIELDS, and CLEAN WATER, where all of the mice live happily!"

The Viking looked at us admiringly. "Ah, are you explorers? If so, maybe you know **ERIK THE RED**, the red-bearded tough-as-Parmesan Viking! Erik is the cousin of the brother of the **uncle** of the sister-in-law of the nephew of my neighbor. He set out a long time ago . . . and we haven't heard any news about him since. I'm Gunter, the VILLAGE CHIEF."

Gunter shook my paw. Holey cheese, he had a **STRONG** grip! "Come, you will be my guests!" he said. "Fabumouse timing — our **VICIOUS VIKING FESTIVAL** begins tomorrow, and you should definitely participate!"

ERIK THE RED
This famous Viking navigator discovered Greenland and settled there in 986 CE with a group of Icelanders. Erik established a community in one of the fjords of the island.

Cheese niblets, I didn't like the sound of that. "Excuse me, Gunter, but what does this festival consist of?"

The Viking chief burst out laughing and gave me a pat on the back that would have knocked an elk off its hooves. "**HO, HO, HO!** You obviously come from far away, foreigners! Everyone around here knows about the Vicious Viking Festival — it's a truly marvemouse event, made up of all sorts of CHALLENGES!"

To help us understand, Gunter laid out a few examples. "There is the TREE TRUNK Challenge (who can lift the biggest tree trunk), the **Courage** Challenge (who can go into a bear's den and make it out alive), the Frozen Herring Challenge (who can swim across a freezing fjord), the Challenge of **No Return** (who can leap from the highest cliff), the DRUMSTICK Challenge (who can eat the most DRUMSTICKS), the **DEADWEIGHT DANCE** Challenge (who can dance with a lady mouse wearing a stone belt), and the SCRAMBLED EGG Challenge (who can gather the most seagull eggs without breaking them). It's a cheeseload of fun, for those who survive. And those who don't make it get a nice **VIKING FUNERAL!**"

Crunchy cheese crisps! I frantically tried to come up with an excuse to turn down Gunter's invitation. I was trying to decide between a very, very contagious stomachache and an unexpected allergy to the Viking air, when Trap squeaked up. "**Yum!** The **DRUMSTICK** Challenge sounds like my kind of competition!"

Yum!

I threw up my paws. We were up to our ears in trouble now!

With no better ideas, we

followed Gunter to the village. All around were houses made of peat and **WOOD** with thatched roofs . . . along with some incredibly ᴇɴᴛʜᴜsɪᴀꜱᴛɪᴄ rodents!

Everyone was busy doing their daily chores and preparing for the challenges! One mouse lifted enormouse **TREE TRUNKS** as if they were made of straw, another did gymnastics with a sack of rocks strapped on his back, and another practiced dancing with a ladymouse who was wearing a belt of ROCKS.

I watched them all, thunderstruck. These rodents were all very large, very strong, and **VERY TOUGH**! How could I possibly compete against them? **RATS!**

I couldn't focus on the fact that I wanted to toss my cheese because just then we ran into Gunter's daughter.

Like a true gentlemouse, I bent down to *kiss* her

paw. But before I knew what was happening, Trap kicked off a chain of **unfortunate** events . . .

Once again, he pulled out his *fascinating essence* and gave me a good **spritz**. Once again, I was enveloped in a terrible stench and a cloud of **flies**. Holey cheese! If that wasn't bad enough, Gunter's daughter began batting her big blue **EYES** at me. "Hi, handsome mouse! My name is Mousehilde. I like your cologne! What is it? Whale oil? Cheese rind? Flea-infested fur? What a fabumouse **fragrance**!"

My cousin had gotten me up to my whiskers in trouble . . . **AGAIN**!

WHEN IS THE WEDDING?

Unfortunately, my troubles were just beginning.

Robota, who had turned herself into a BROOCH on my Viking cape, pinched me in a fit of jealousy, yelling, "You horrible flirt!"

Hearing those words, Mousehilde was offended — she thought I'd said them! Before I could explain, she gave me a smack on the snout that made me spin around like a top. Then she stormed off.

Heeeelp!

You rat!

At that point, I was pawsitive that the village chief was going to turn me into mouse **marmalade**. Squeak!

Instead, Gunter began to chuckle under his mustache, rubbing his paws together. "Good, good, good. I was worried about my little one. She has a **TEMPER** and, until now, she has refused all suitors. But she likes you, mouse! So when is the wedding?"

I was about to respond that we wouldn't even squeak of a wedding, but Thea kicked my **RigHt** paw and whispered in my ear, "If I were you, I wouldn't refuse!"

Trap kicked my **left** paw and squeaked, "My cousin would be thrilled to get engaged to your daughter, chief!"

I couldn't believe my ears! "I'm not planning to get engaged or **married** today!" I burst out.

The chief narrowed his eyes. "If you disappoint

my little one, I will make you into mouse marmalade — Viking's honor!"

Suddenly, the rest of Mousehilde's family surrounded us — her **mother**, *aunt*, great-aunt, cousin, great-grandmother, and sister. Oh, for the love of cheese! They all yelled, "Who is marrying our little Mousehilde?"

Every one of them looked me up and down, checked my puny biceps, and poked my jiggly BELLY.

The great-grandmother peered at me doubtfully. "Really? This mouse?"

The *grandmother* sighed. "He doesn't seem to have very many muscles."

The mother shrugged. "He has a soft belly!"

The aunt grinned. "I think he's kind of cute!"

The great-aunt added, "He's not bad!"

The **cousin** squeaked, "He seems smart."

And the sister concluded, "He has mousetastic

whiskers! If Mousehilde doesn't marry him, I **WiLL**!"

Luckily, Gunter interrupted. "**Enough!** In order to marry my little cheese niblet, this mouse has to earn it. Tomorrow, he will win the Vicious Viking Festival, or I will turn him into mouse **marmalade**!"

He stared straight into my eyes. Squeak! "If I were you, I would start **training**! Don't disappoint my daughter, or you'll be nothing but a pile of cheesecrumbs when I'm finished with you!"

Then he boomed, "**Bjorn! Gunnar! Magnus!** Get over here!"

Three enormouse mice scurried over to us. "Here we are, boss! You called? Who do you need us to demolish?"

The chief responded, "Good, good, good! You don't need to demolish anyone . . . for now. But I need you to train this one, here. He's not much of a **musclemouse**, but tomorrow he needs to win **all** the competitions! If he wins — that is, if he can even survive — he is going to **MARRY** my Mousehilde."

They nodded. "Boss, leave it to us. We'll make a real Viking out of him in just one day!"

Then they grabbed me by my **EARS** and the **TAIL** and dragged me away. "Hey, careful!" I yelped. "Didn't you hear him? He said I have to **survive!**"

MAGNUS

We'll help!

BJORN

GUNNAR

But they didn't loosen their grip until we got outside the village. It was time to start my *TRAINING* — whether I wanted to or not!

First, Bjorn brought me to a pile of **TREE TRUNKS** so he could teach me how to lift them. He pointed at the biggest and ordered, "Lift that one!"

I tried, using all of my mousely strength. I turned **purple** with the effort, but it didn't even budge a millimeter. So Bjorn had me gradually try with smaller and smaller trunks. When I finally

Begin with that one!

Grrrr . . .

Try this one!

I can do it . . .

got to the lightest one, I muttered, "I can do it . . . I can do it . . . I can — "

With an enormouse effort, I was able to lift it a half inch, then — **BANG**!

I fell on the ground, exhausted.

At that point, Bjorn grabbed a **BROOM** from a mouse cleaning the henhouse, shoved it into my paw, and said, "Try this."

So I trained to lift weights using a **filthy**, stinky broom. I was surrounded by flies — double-twisted rat tails, how embarrassing!

THE COURAGE
CHALLENGE

Help!
A bear!

THE FROZEN
HERRING CHALLENGE

Brrrrr!

THE CHALLENGE
OF NO RETURN

I'm too fond of my fur!

The rest of my training wasn't much better. I'll just say that I did not demonstrate that I was capable of doing the COURAGE Challenge (I'm allergic to wild bear fur, especially if the bear is ferocious and hungry), or **swimming** in freezing water (I went down like a stone), or **diving** off the cliffs (I am mousetastically afraid of heights).

I hoped to do better in the **Deadweight Dance** Challenge, but . . . I had some trouble spinning the local maidens. They were so much **BIGGER** than me! Even the DRUMSTICK Challenge was a huge flop. Trap, on the other paw, kept up with the best rodents in the village! (I have to admit, he is truly a champion eater.) I thought I could handle the Scrambled Egg Challenge, but . . . I broke every last egg I collected!

SQUEAK, I WAS HOPELESS!!!

HERE IS A REAL VIKING!

The next morning at dawn, all the Vikings met in a clearing just outside the walls of the village. The village chief signaled for the official start of the festival, striking his shield with his ax.

CRACK!

The competitors got their tails into gear in the different challenges, while everyone around cheered for their FAVORITES.

Before I began, Trap whispered, "I strongly suggest that you try to concentrate. Don't disappoint me. I BET everything on you!"

Cheese niblets, what was he squeaking about?

Astonished, I asked him, "EVERYTHING? What do you mean? We don't **have** anything! What did you bet?"

Trap shrugged. "You're such a cheesebrain sometimes, cousin! I **BET** the Whisker Wafter, obviously!"

I wanted to pull out my whiskers! "Why did you do that?! You know that I'm no musclemouse! We'll lose the **whisker wafter**, and we'll never get back to New Mouse City!"

Just then, something truly **unexpected** happened. From the bottom of the clearing came a group of Vikings, fully armed. In seconds, they had us **SURROUNDED**.

An enormouse Viking with red **hair**, thick WHISKERS, and a long, BRAIDED beard planted himself in front of Gunter. "You are surrounded! What are you going to do, Gunter? Do you want to surrender, or do you want to FIGHT?"

Gunter growled, "How dare you, Leifrat?"

Without thinking, I stepped between the two,

holding up my paws and trying to make peace. "Stop! We can find a **SOLUTION**!"

Everyone looked at me, surprised. "What solution? We'll have a good battle! The mice who live, win. The mice who are crushed, lose!"

Moldy mozzarella, were they **SERIOUS**? "But if you fight each other, many mice could get hurt!"

"What do you suggest, Geronimord?" Gunter asked.

I stepped closer to him and **WHISPERED**, "You could . . . psst, psst . . . challenge . . ."

He clapped a large paw on my back (which pushed me down into the ground like a **nail**!), then strangled me in a suffocating hug. "Good mouse! I am **happy** that you're going to be my son-in-law!"

I tried to catch my breath. "But I never said that I wanted to **marry** your daughter . . ."

He burst into laughter. "What a funny rodent! **Everyone** wants to marry my daughter!"

Gunter turned to the ENEMY chief. "Leifrat, here's my proposal: We will not battle each other, but we will each nominate a champion to compete in a challenge. Whoever wins the competition wins everything! It won't be a challenge of

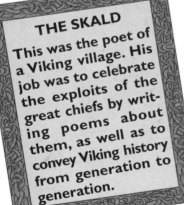

THE SKALD

This was the poet of a Viking village. His job was to celebrate the exploits of the great chiefs by writing poems about them, as well as to convey Viking history from generation to generation.

THE THING

When the Vikings needed to make an important decision for the community or vote on laws, they held an assembly, called a "thing." Any free Vikings could participate and express their opinions.

strength, but of **intelligence**! Do you agree? Our champion will be . . . *Geronimord*!"

Leifrat burst into laughter, holding his belly. "Ha, ha! That flabby mozzarella slab is your champion? We'll win for sure!" He clapped his paws and yelled, "The competition is on! Come forward, my son Rolf, our skald — or poet, for you cheesebrains out there!"

THE CHALLENGE OF INTELLIGENCE!

Mice from both sides of the challenge sat in a circle in the CLEARING, murmuring, "This is going to be fabumouse!"

Robota, who was still attached to my cape, decided to start talking to me again. (She had been giving me the silent treatment because she was so jealous of Mousehilde!)

Dearest!

"Dearest, don't be scared, I will help you!"

I smiled. "Thanks, Robota — I think I'm really going to need you this time!"

The challenge began, and **ROLF** was up first. The poet went to the center of the circle and began to recite a complicated legend . . .

When he was done, everyone applauded

A long time ago, in frozen Iceland, lived a warrior princess named Brunhilde. Prince Gunther fell in love with her, but she only wanted to marry someone who was even stronger and more courageous than she was. Gunther asked his friend Sigfried, a great warrior, for help. Sigfried disguised himself as Gunther, winning the duel and Brunhilde's heart (on Gunther's behalf).

Though Brunhilde was angry at being tricked, Gunther and Brunhilde went on to be married and lived happily together for many years.

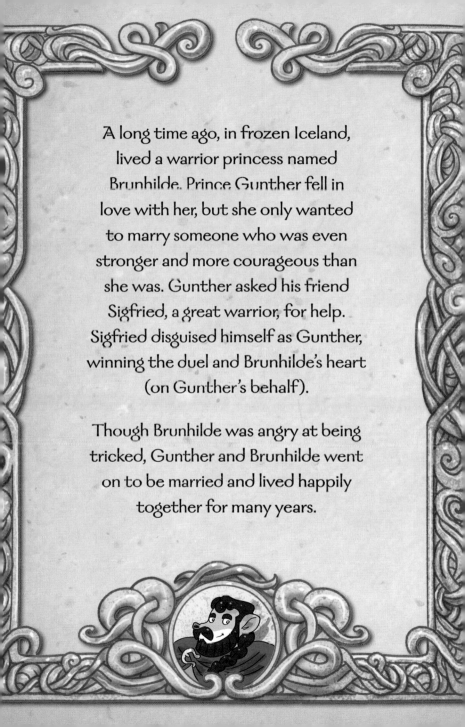

enthusiastically. Curdled cheesecakes, how would I follow that? I walked to the center of the circle with trembling *knees*, wobbling **whiskers**, and a mouth drier than aged Parmesan. I'm really very **shy**, and squeaking in public makes me tremendmousely anxious! And this time, the fate of the village and the Whisker Wafter depended on me. **Holey cheese, what a disaster!**

Luckily, Benjamin stepped up to me, grabbed my paw, and said, "Uncle, don't worry. No one tells better stories than you!" Thea, Trap, and Bugsy Wugsy were all nodding in agreement.

Tell stories . . . tell stories . . . tell stories . . . So I began to tell a story . . .

Tell stories . . . tell stories . . . tell stories . . .

Luckily, everyone liked my story, too! Before I knew it, Rolf and I were tied!

Rolf, confident that he was the only one around who could read and write in multiple languages,

Once upon a time, a mouse journeyed from a faraway land. He wasn't courageous, nor was he a musclemouse. He was just a regular rodent, like me!

He set out in search of a precious ring that had enormouse powers. It was said that this ring would save his land.

One day, that mouse was caught in a terrible storm and ended up in an unknown land inhabited by fabumousely courageous Viking rodents. They were tough warriors, tough blacksmiths and farmers, tough big mice and tough little mice. Tough mothers and tough children, tough aunts and tough uncles, they were tough grandpas . . . and even the tough grandmas carried axes under their skirts!

One day, that mouse wrote a story about them. And that story was told and retold for years and years. Thanks to him, everyone knew all about that infamousely tough Viking tribe!

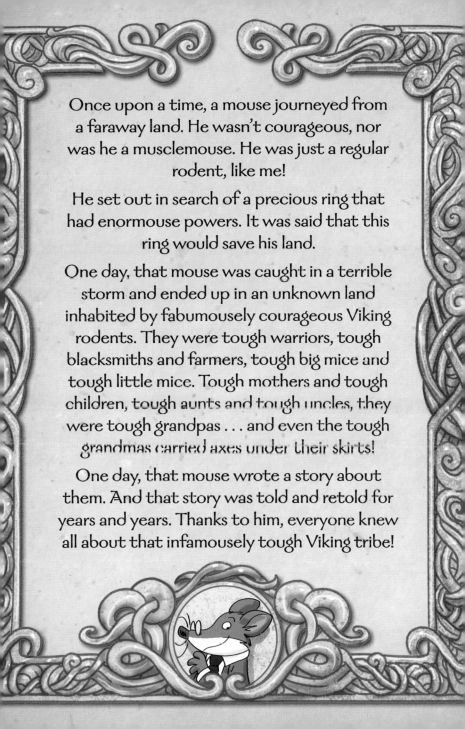

proposed a new challenge — we would compete by reading text in the **runic alphabet**!

I was up first. I had to decipher the sentence:

"Poor me, I am in trouble!"

Luckily, Robota knows all the languages in the **world**. With her help, the translation was easy cheesy.

Hey, wait just one whisker-licking minute! Rolf had also written, "Foolish Geronimord!" **THAT RAT!**

Next, Rolf gave me a **riddle**: "What never dies but becomes old in a month?"

Poor me!

Try to read this!

Runic Alphabet

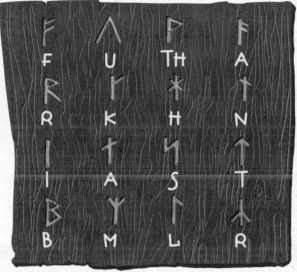

Runic writing was invented by Germanic populations and became popular in Scandinavia around 200 CE. The Vikings adopted a modified version of the runic alphabet; they only used sixteen of the twenty-four original runes. The runes were most often engraved with a blade or an awl on wooden boards, blocks of stone, pieces of bone, metal, or leather. Familiarity with the runic alphabet was a privilege reserved for the most important families, who had to read in order to govern their people. Writing in the runic alphabet was most often used for administrative functions or to preserve the memory of relatives that passed away.

I didn't have a cheesecrumb of a clue. But clever Benjamin whispered in my ear.

"**The moon!**" I exclaimed.

Then it was my turn to challenge Rolf, so I proposed another riddle, the most difficult one I could think of. "What doesn't lessen when it falls but increases?"

Rolf grinned. "Easy — the **FOG**!" He countered, "What makes everyone tremble without threatening?"

Cheese and crackers, this one was tricky! I thought and thought and thought, but I couldn't come up with a good answer. I was about to tie my tail in knots when, suddenly, a **thunderstorm** broke out and rain began to pour out of the sky!

The water soaked me from snout to tail, and the cold wind made me shiver. **Brrr!** Just then, I knew the answer. "I've got it — the **COLD**!"

Help Geronimo Win the Riddle Competition!

1. These have big hats but no heads to cover. They have only one foot but no shoes to wear. What are they?

2. These wear many different colors, but when they get cold, they undress. What are they?

3. This carries its house on its shoulders to travel the mountains and the valleys. Do you know what it's called?

4. These arrive at night, even if they aren't called. During the day they disappear, but no one steals them. What are they?

5. When this passes through, everyone takes off their hats. This has teeth but doesn't bite. What is it?

6. This has a hole in its head but can also make many holes. What is it?

7. You can plant this, but it won't grow. It has a head but can't think. What is it?

1. Mushrooms 2. Trees 3. A snail 4. Stars 5. A comb 6. A needle 7. A nail

HOORAY FOR THE NEWLYWEDS!

Once the thunderstorm passed, Rolf and I kept taking turns with the riddles . . . but after many rounds, we were still TIED! Squeak, this competition would never end!

Gunther had a new proposal. "Let's have a poetry competition! Whoever composes the most BEAUTIFUL POEM in honor of Mousehilde, my very **beautiful daughter**, will win!"

He winked at me and whispered, "It should be easy for you to compose a poem about Mousehilde — after all, aren't you her FIANCÉ?"

I threw my paws into the air and squeaked, "I am not her fiancé! And I am not a poet!"

But I had to WIN the challenge. What else could I do?

Rolf was up first this time. He got down on one knee and looked deep into Mousehilde's eyes as he recited,

> Oh, sweet Mousehilde:
> Your eyes are the color of the sky
> And your hair the color of the grain.
> Nothing could stop me, by and by —
> Not wind, nor ice, nor sleet, nor rain —
> For declaring my love to be over the moon.
> I'll stop at nothing to be your groom!

I noticed that Mousehilde was **BLUSHING**. Rancid ricotta, she seemed to like Rolf's poem!

At last, it was my turn. I stood in front of Mousehilde with one paw over my heart. I cleared my throat, looked her in the eye, and . . . I had nothing to squeak! absolutely nothing!

All I could think was that, if I won, I would be **FORCED** to marry her! Rats!

After a few seconds, I was finally able to open

my mouth — and the **cheesiest** poem of all time spilled out!

> *Oh, my beautiful Viking,*
>
> *You remind me of a . . . fish.*
>
> *I hope this poem is to your liking,*
>
> *Because your . . . happiness . . . is all I wish.*
>
> *I get confused and sometimes s-stutter,*
>
> *When you are in the room*
>
> *Because . . . um . . . it often makes me shudder*
>
> *To think of our marital doom!*

I didn't even finish before Mouschilde stood up, walked up to me, and **SLAPPED** me right across the snout. I **spun** around like a top!

How dare you?

Oh, my beautiful Viking, you remind me of a . . . fish!

She squeaked, "Cheesebrain! You aren't my fiancé anymore — I don't know what I ever found so fascinating about you! Rolf is a real Viking, **strong** but also ROMANTIC!"

I tried to apologize. "Mousehilde, forgive me. I didn't mean to offend you! I can't make my *heart* feel something it doesn't." I sighed. "You and I wouldn't be HAPPY together. But it seems like you and Rolf might . . ."

Just then, Gunter approached, twirling his ax. Squeak! "Rodent, you disappointed my daughter! I'm going to make mouse **marmalade** out of you!"

I held up a paw. "Wait a minute, please! I have an idea that may bring peace to your village: let Mousehilde marry Rolf. Their *marriage* will unite the two villages into one strong force!"

Gunter set down his ax, musing, "Hmmm! Thunder, lightning, and axes, this is a *fabumouse*

idea! And I have to admit, I'm glad that you aren't going to be my future son-in-law . . ."

Then he turned to Rolf. "As for you, you had better not DISAPPOINT my daughter — otherwise I'll make *you* into mouse marmalade! Understand?"

Since everyone was already gathered together, we celebrated the *wedding* right there! A day that began with the threat of war ended with a party, celebrating the union of two hearts and two villages!

Today we marry!

I'm so happy!

Do You Believe in Love at First Sight?

The wedding reception was beautiful, with singing, dancing, and poetry.

Trap especially liked the food. He rubbed his belly happily. "**BURP!** I love the Viking life! If we didn't have to go back to New Mouse City to patent my *fascinating essence*, I would think about staying here!"

I couldn't help laughing. "You and your *fascinating essence*! That stuff keeps getting me into **messes**!"

"But that just proves how well it works!" said Trap. "Even for you, the least charming rodent I know! If you hadn't been such a horrible poet, you would be marrying the daughter of the Viking chief! Isn't that MARVEMOUSE?"

I responded, **exasperated**, "No, it's not marvemouse! I don't want a rodent to fall in love with me because of your extra-stinky spray! I'm a romantic mouse, and I'm still searching for my soul mate! I believe in true love, love at first sight . . ."

At that point, Robota spoke up from the folds of my cape. "Ah, so you're still looking for your soul mate? You mean it isn't me? You said that you want to be STRUCK by love at first sight? What do you think about this kind of strike?"

She suddenly zapped me with a flurry of blue

Take that!
Zap!

Squeeeeeak!

shocks that fried all of my whiskers. Oh, for the love of cheese — what a day!

Just then Gunter got up, slammed his large 𝕞𝕦𝕘 on the table, and thundered, "Quiet — it's my turn to squeak! I just want to thank the rodent who helped us to avoid a bloody **_battle_** today. He even managed to help my little one find the right *groom*!"

Emotional, he blew his nose on my tunic. "Pfffff! Oh, I'm so happy!"

Then he clapped a huge paw on my shoulder. "Ask me for anything, Geronimord, and you shall have it!"

"Thank you, Gunter," I said with a smile. "But I don't need anything from you. I already have everything a mouse could ask for. Plus, you've given me a precious gift — YOUR FRiENDSHiP!"

Everyone applauded as I sat down.

Thea leaned over and whispered in my ear. "I just found out that wedding receptions around here can last for **DAYS**. You should ask Gunter if we can leave right away — we have to get back to our mission. Mouse Island is in danger!"

My sister was right. It was time to return to the **whisker wafter**!

I had to admit, the idea of leaving made me SAD. I was fond of our new Viking friends! They were strong (maybe too strong!), decisive (maybe

too decisive!), tough (definitely too tough!), but also sincere and loyal.

I got to my paws again and said solemnly, "Gunter, I do have one thing to ask you: would you permit me and my family to leave this marvemouse banquet? We need to *get our tails in gear*! Our village is in danger, and we are on a mission to save it. A long and dangerous journey awaits us."

Gunter seemed **UPSET**, but then he smiled. "Normally I would consider that kind of request to be rude, but I understand. If you have a mission to complete, you must go! Who knows, maybe one day we'll hear your adventures told by famous poets . . ."

Gunter **StRaNgLeD** me with one last Viking hug. Then we said our good-byes and headed back to the Whisker Wafter.

EVERYONE STOP, I'LL DO IT!

This time, I had to get to the **COMMAND** center before Trap. I was tired of going to the wrong time periods, and I couldn't handle any more fur-raising adventures! I wanted to be sure we were headed for the age of *King Solomon*.

So I scampered to the control room, squeaking at the top of my lungs, "Everyone stop, I'll do it!"

But just as I was about to reach the computer,

Everyone stop! I'll do it!

Oof!

Argh!

Trap **TRIPPED** me! I landed snoutdown on the floor of the ship.

Faster than a mouse on a cheese hunt, Trap grabbed a random cube of TIME FUEL and shoved it into the container. BAM!

BAM!

Done!

Before anyone could squeak, the Whisker Wafter began to vibrate. There was a flash of light, and we found ourselves **ROCKING** on the electromagnetic waves of the Ocean of Infinite Time!

Holey cheese, where in time were we going to wind up now?

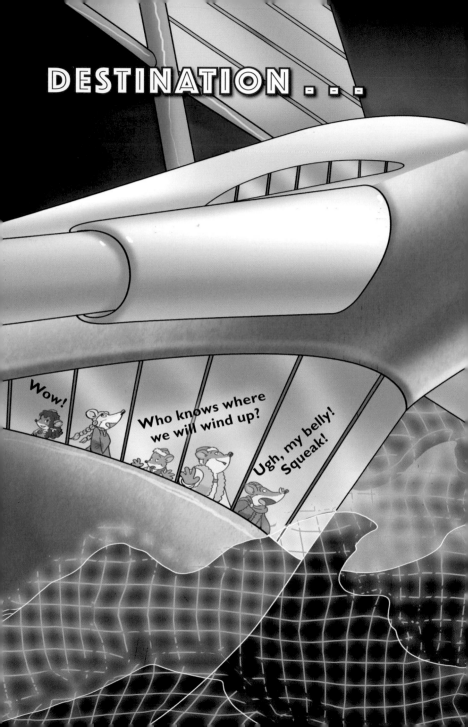

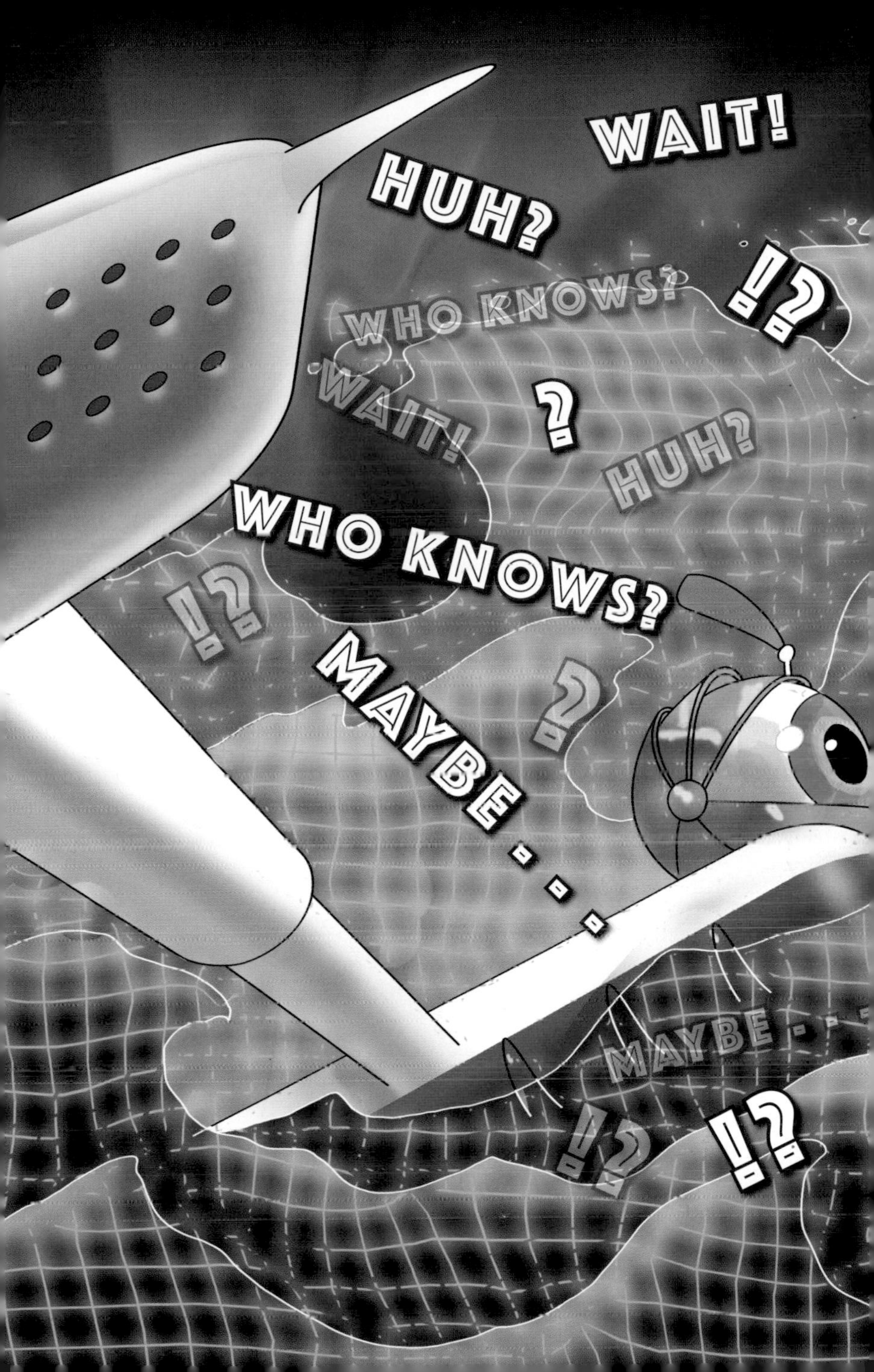
WAIT!
HUH?
WHO KNOWS?
!?
WAIT!
?
HUH?
WHO KNOWS?
!?
MAYBE...
?
MAYBE...
!?
!?

I didn't get a chance to ask any questions, because the Ocean of Infinite Time was stormy today! The electromagnetic waves were very high, and the Whisker Wafter began to sway **UP** and **DOWN**. Rats!

Bugsy Wugsy, Benjamin, and Thea threw their paws in the air, squeaking that it was much better than a **roller coaster**!

Me? Yup, I was ready to **toss my cheese** again!

If that wasn't bad enough, Trap wagged a paw in my face. "Cousin, look what you've done! Remember that I am the boss! So I command, and you obey! I type, and you stay and watch! I drive the Whisker Wafter, and you are a passenger!"

I didn't even try to defend myself. I didn't have the strength.

In the meantime, **Robota** pulled me by the cape, trying to get my attention. She wanted me

to help her organize the **NOTES** in the onboard diary.

"Dearest, I **MIXED UP** all the files! You'll have dictate everything to me from the beginning, starting with the day we left."

Oh, crusty cheddar chunks! I escaped to the deck of the Whisker Wafter. I needed some peace and quiet, and I hoped the *fresh air* would help with my time sickness. But as I stepped onto the deck, an enormouse wave washed over the ship. I

I'm too fond
of my fur!

slipped overboard — now I was hanging on
to the bow of the Whisker Wafter with just
one paw! **SQUEEEEEEAK!**
I'm too fond of my fur!

I was about to lose my grip and thought
I would be lost forever in the Ocean of
Infinite Time, when suddenly there was a
FLASH OF LIGHT. Holey cheese, I
was safe! We had arrived, but... **where**?

I peered around. It looked like we were
off the coast of an **island** in the
Mediterranean . . .

THE ANCIENT ISLAND OF CRETE

ARE YOU HAPPY, CHEESEPUFF?

Robota helped me down from the bow of the Whisker Wafter, which had transformed into a light merchant **Ship**. "Do you want to know what age we are in? I'll pull it up immediately!"

She quickly used her **SCANNER** to examine the three-dimensional shape of the hull of the Whisker Wafter and the material on the sail, and then pronounced, "We are in **Crete** in 1700 BCE! Are you happy, cheesepuff?"

What type of mice are the Cretans?

I responded, "Um, I don't know. What type of mice are the Cretans? Are they . . . **DANGEROUS**?"

We are in Crete!

We joined the others and hurried to change clothes.

CRETE AND THE MINOAN CIVILIZATION

Between approximately 2600 BCE and 1150 BCE, the Minoan civilization developed on the island of Crete. It was a refined civilization and engaged in commercial and cultural exchanges with the nearby East and West.

POTTERY

The painted pottery from this era highlights the elegance of the Minoan civilization. Geometric figures, animals, and flowers wind beautifully around vases and jars!

WRITING

Phaistos Disc

The oldest Cretan writing, similar to hieroglyphics, has not been completely deciphered by modern scholars. The Phaistos Disc, a clay disc covered with this writing and dating back to 1700 BCE, is a notable exception — it was decrypted in 2014.

Linear B

Later, Minoan hieroglyphics were replaced by signs associated with letters. The Minoans developed one writing form called Linear A, and later another called Linear B. These are the primary Minoan writings that have been deciphered to date.

MINOAN FASHION

What we know of Minoan fashion is that it was especially refined. Precious fabrics, elaborate hairstyles, jewelry, and jewels made the men and women of the time look very elegant!

Geronimeo

Theanna

Bugso Wugso

FEMININE FASHION

Minoan women wore clothes with short sleeves and long, swaying skirts, often flounced and decorated with intricate patterns. They complemented this look with elaborate hairstyles, jewelry, and sometimes hats.

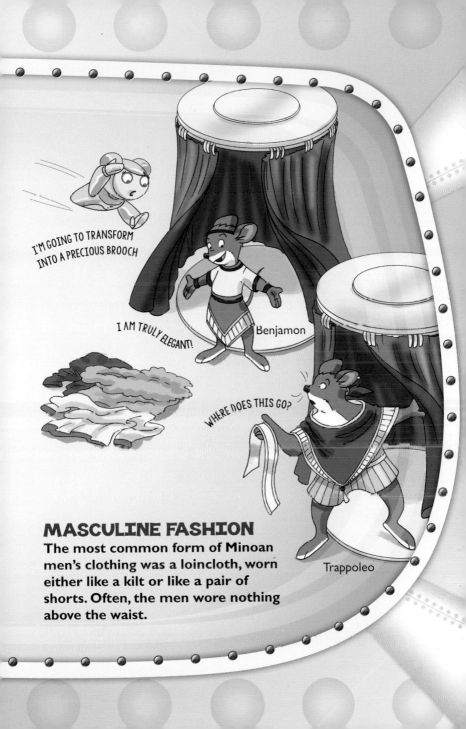

MASCULINE FASHION

The most common form of Minoan men's clothing was a loincloth, worn either like a kilt or like a pair of shorts. Often, the men wore nothing above the waist.

While we put the finishing touches on our costumes, Robota (who had once again transformed herself into a fancy brooch) began to give us a cheeseload of INFORMATION about the Minoans. She told us that they were peaceful, refined rodents who loved art and NATURE. Relieved, I proposed that we take a trip around the island. I was jumping out of my fur to see the famous **Palace of Knossos**!

This time, though, I was going to confiscate the *fascinating essence* from Trap. I'd had enough of his treacherous spritzes! I slipped the bottle in my tunic and exclaimed, "I'll hang on to this. I can't handle any more rodents tripping over their paws to marry me!"

I'll take this.

We stepped off the ship — and were immediately caught up in a cheering and very **colorful** crowd!

Where was everyone **RUNNING**?

The only way to find out was to join in! As we ran, Bugsy Wugsy and Benjamin began to complain. "Putrid Parmesan! How much further?"

To distract them, I began to tell the story of the **MINOTAUR**, who was said by Cretan legend to live in the Labyrinth. The mouselets forgot all about their tired paws until we arrived at the Palace of Knossos. Only then did I understand why there was such an enormouse crowd — it was a holiday! Something was definitely about to happen in the immense courtyard of the palace . . . **BUT WHAT**?

THE MINOTAUR
This legend tells the tale of the Minotaur, half bull and half man, which King Minos confined in the labyrinth at the Palace of Knossos. Every year, children and maidens were given to the beast as food, until Theseus was able to kill him, with the help of the king's daughter, Ariadne.

HARVEST FESTIVAL

It is believed that, every year, the Minoans organized a large harvest festival to celebrate the year's crops. During this event, a court likely crossed city streets crowded with people: first came four singers, followed by a musician and a dancer, then a large crowd of young farmers (led by the landowners). The youth waved bundles of wheat and bouquets of poppies, and jumped and danced cheerfully.

GREAT GOLDEN HORN OF THE SACRED BULL!

As we arrived in the courtyard, an enormouse crowd rumbled all around us, waiting for something to happen . . .

Finally, mice began to squeak, "Here he is! He's coming! He's coming!"

Benjamin and Bugsy Wugsy looked up at me curiously. "Uncle G, do you see anything? Who's coming?"

I stood on my **tiptoes**, but all I could see were the necks and ears of other rodents in the crowd. Rats!

I grabbed the **mouselets** by the paws and pushed ahead to the first row, SQUEAKING, "Ahem . . . excuse me . . . excuse me . . . pardon . . . can I please pass?"

The mice around us just kept saying, "Here he is! Here he is! He's coming!"

As we worked our way through the crowd, being careful not to step on tails or stomp on paws, Bugsy Wugsy HOPPED next to me. She yanked on my sleeve and shrieked, "Who's coming? Who? Who? Whooooooooo?"

When we reached the first row, we could see a procession of young mice, dancing and playing music with bunches of wheat, tulips, and ripe fruit in their paws. For a second, I thought that

everyone had been waiting for them — but I was tremendmousely wrong!

The procession continued into the castle, but the crowd began rumbling excitedly again, "Here he comes, he's coming, he's coooming!"

Just then, a bunch of things happened at once:

Trap came up behind us, bumping into me. "Hey, Cousin, let me see! Who's arriving?"

I **fell** forward, **tripped** on my own feet, and tumbled right into the middle of the courtyard.

From my tunic, Robota yelled, "Be careful of the **bullfight**!* Watch out for the bull!"

---

* The bullfight was a show consisting of a fight between an athlete and a bull, which was extremely popular in ancient times.

Shaking my snout in a daze, I said, "Watch out for the . . . **WHAT**?"

But I didn't have time to get a response — because an enormouse black **bull** was galloping straight toward me! Holey cheese!

To avoid being riddled with holes like a piece of Swiss cheese by its sharp **horns**, I grabbed the horns with my paws and held on for dear life. The bull gave a **shake**, and I was launched into the air, doing a spectacular **somersault**

over his back. **Squeeeeeeak!**

Don't ask me how, but I landed perfectly on my paws! **WHEW!**

The audience burst into cheers.

"Great golden horn of the sacred bull, what an athlete!"

"Bravo! Beautiful bull leap!"

"Encore!"

When I understood what had happened, I muttered, "N-n-no encore, for the love of cheese!"

Suddenly, everything went **BLACK** and I **FAINTED**. The last thing I saw was a cloud of that rat-munching *fascinating essence* surrounding me.

Cheesy creampuffs, I had **broken** the bottle!

Then I began to dream . . .

THE BULL LEAP
This was a stunt performed by young Cretan athletes. They ran toward the bull, grabbed it by the horns, and launched into a somersault through the air, landing behind the animal.

"BRAVO!" "ENCORE!" "GREAT GOLDEN HORN OF THE SACRED BULL, WHAT AN ATHLETE!"

I DREAMED THAT . . .

In my dream, I found myself in front of a very beautiful young mouse with long brown hair gathered up in an elaborate hairstyle. She gave me a shake. "Hurry, Geronimeo — wake up and follow me! I'll show you the way!"

Fascinated by her large **EYES** and graceful gestures, I said, "Sure, sure — but tell me, miss, where are we going?"

"To meet him, of course!" she replied, surprised.

Ouch!

Hurry, Geronimeo, follow me!

I didn't have a cheesecrumb of a clue about who **he** was, but I didn't dare ask. I didn't want this fascinating rodent to think I was a total **cheesebrain**! "Of course! I came just to . . . ahem . . . meet him!"

She batted her long dark eyelashes. "Oh Geronimeo, you are the **HERO** I have been waiting for!"

Blushing with embarrassment, I stuttered, "Oh, no . . . I'm not really a hero!"

She smiled. "You're heroic and modest! What a marvemouse rodent!"

She led me to the entrance of a long, dark hallway. She tied a red string on my tail, gave me a kiss on the tip of my snout, and said, "Go, my hero, and come back a winner! But, above all, come back! All of the other heroes have been squished. To find the exit, just follow the RED STRING!"

ARIADNE'S THREAD
According to Greek mythology, Theseus, the son of the king of Athens, fought against the Minotaur in Crete. He was able to escape the labyrinth with the help of Ariadne, the daughter of Cretan king Minos. She gave him a ball of thread that he used to mark his path in the labyrinth, so he could follow it back to escape easily!

My head was spinning and my knees were trembling with fear. I set paw into the very dark, very long, and very twisted **corridor**.

I walked for what seemed like forever! I turned **RIGHT**, then **LEFT**, **RIGHT**, and then **RIGHT** again . . . to the **LEFT** . . . to the **RIGHT** . . . until I had no idea where I was! Rats!

In the meantime, a **FLURRY** of questions scurried through my mind. Who was in here? Why had the other heroes been squished? Why didn't I ask the lovely mouse her name? Why did I let her lead me into this?

I didn't know the answers to any of the questions, except for the last one. I had let the fascinating rodent lead me to the maze because . . . I was an enormouse fool!

Just then, I spotted something terrifying up ahead. It made a loud sound that cut through my thoughts. "MOOOOOOOOOOOOOOOOOOOO!"

Chattering cheddar — this was truly FUR-RAISING! Who could have made a noise like that?

The ground began to shake:

BADABAM!
BADABAM!
BADABAM!

Who was coming toward me? I didn't have to wait long to find out. A second later, I was snout-to-snout with one of the most TERRIFYING mythical creatures of all time — the MINOTAUR!

I SPUN on my paws and began to run as fast as I could in the

Squeak! I'm too fond of my fur!

opposite direction. The terrible creature followed me, yelling, "Rodent, you are small, but you seem tasty! I think you will make a yummy appetizer! **MOOOOOOOOOOOOO!**"

I was so **TERRIFIED** that I forgot all about the string attached to my tail! I began to run in circles, followed by the Minotaur. Just when I thought I would surely be caught and gobbled up, his hooves became tangled in my string. He fell with his nose to the ground, hitting me on the head with a tremendmouse crash.

BAAAAAAANG!

Moldy mozzarella! Everything went black.

Then I heard voices calling to me . . . and I woke up from the dream.

Holey cheese, I had dreamed that I was Theseus, facing off against the Minotaur!

"GERONIMEO! GERONIMEO! WAKE UP!"
"IT'S TIME FOR US TO GET MARRIED!"
"NO, I'M GOING TO MARRY HIM!"
"PAWS OFF! I SAW HIM FIRST!"

AN ENORMOUSE CLOUD OF FLIES

When I opened my eyes, I found myself surrounded by a cloud of FLIES. When I fell, I had broken the bottle of *fascinating essence* and it had SPILLED all over me! Rancid ricotta, what rotten luck!

The worst part was that Trap's perfume had already taken effect. I was surrounded by a crowd of lady mice who were all FIGHTING — about

Paws off!

I'm going to marry him!

No, I'm going to marry him!

who would get to marry me!

I had no choice — I had to **ESCAPE**! Not knowing which direction to go in, I whispered, "Robota, help me, I must find a way out of here! Tell me how!"

She responded, "*Of course, my cheesepuff!* We have to get rid of those terrible flirts. After all, if anyone here is going to marry you, it's me!"

I was about to answer back that I didn't plan to marry anyone today (especially not a little robot), but she went on. "Let's not talk about it now — there's no time, and those ladies are after you! Follow my instructions: I have the map of the whole Palace of Knossos in my memory. If we go through the palace, we'll find a shortcut behind it that should lead us back to the Whisker Wafter."

Robota began **directing** me toward the palace. "Run this way! Now that way! Turn right,

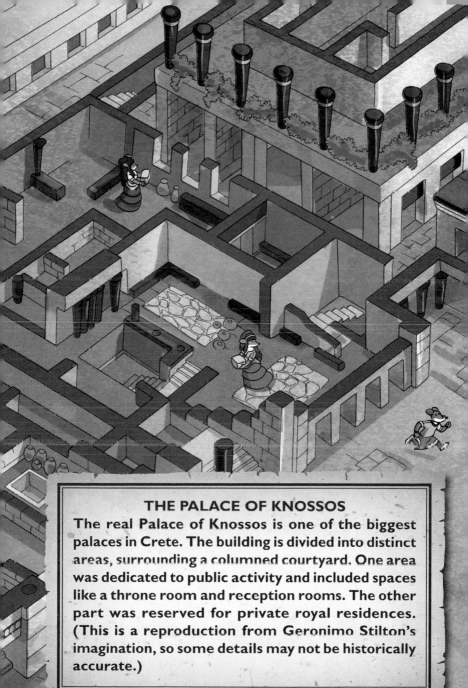

THE PALACE OF KNOSSOS

The real Palace of Knossos is one of the biggest palaces in Crete. The building is divided into distinct areas, surrounding a columned courtyard. One area was dedicated to public activity and included spaces like a throne room and reception rooms. The other part was reserved for private royal residences. (This is a reproduction from Geronimo Stilton's imagination, so some details may not be historically accurate.)

no, left! Go straight! Turn around!"

In the meantime, Thea, Bugsy Wugsy, Trap, and Benjamin tried to sidetrack my many SUITORS, giving them random directions. "Are you looking for Geronimeo? He went that way!"

"No, I saw him **over there**!"

"Take this hallway and turn **right**!"

"Remember to go down the staircase to the **left**!"

"Then go **up**!"

"No, go **down**!"

Following Robota's directions, I was running the

opposite way in search of the shortcut. Great balls of mozzarella, the Palace of Knossos was enormouse! It felt like a real **labyrinth**!

I ran across the kitchen, where a delicious **ROAST** was cooking (and I burned my tail on the **hearth**, youch!). Then I crept into the throne room, where a royal **hearing** was taking place (and I was

What a hit!

chased out by guards carrying **axes**, squeak!). I was out of breath — but I couldn't stop now!

I got my tail in gear and scampered along a corridor of brightly painted columns . . . until I slipped on the stairs and bonked my head on a column, cracking the plaster. Youch! I got back on my paws and soon found myself in a **BATHROOM**, complete with a bathtub and a soaking mouse. I was so surprised that I accidentally stepped in a puddle of water and slipped — again!

With ladies and armed **GUARDS** still on my tail, I ducked into one of the huge storerooms cluttered with **JARS** of oil — but I crashed

into a jar, and my fur got covered in **olive oil**! This time my clumsiness turned out to be lucky, because when the guards tried to grab me, I was able to slip right out of their paws and head for the **whisker wafter**. What a mousetastic escape!

A STRATEGIC RETREAT!

Since I was the first one on the Whisker Wafter this time around, I got to the **CONTROL ROOM** first. I had to take charge before Trap sent us OFF COURSE again!

I headed for the main keyboard and quickly searched for the cube labeled King Solomon, 960 BCE!

As soon as Thea, Trap, Bugsy Wugsy, and Benjamin came aboard, I put the cube into

Finally, we'll go visit King Solomon!

the container and pushed the SEND button. Holey cheese — I had done it!

Trap, always a troublemaker, tried to stop me — but he was too late!

The Whisker Wafter began to vibrate, there was the usual flash of light, and again we set off across the Ocean of Infinite Time!

Luckily, this time it was dead calm! We decided to enjoy the ride and head up to the deck to admire the mouserific landscape. Cheese niblets, it was beautiful!

While Bugsy Wugsy and Benjamin told JOKES next to the pool, Trap sprawled out on a chair and began to snore. Thea put a rejuvenating mask on her fur. And me? I was forced to suffer through hours of Robota's nonstop chatter!

"My cheesepuff, now that I have saved you, we should start planning the **WEDDING**. Lucky for you, I have already given it a lot of thought, from the dress to the reception *menu*! Isn't that wonderful?"

Just as I thought I might fly out of my fur, there was the usual FLASH OF BRIGHT WHITE LIGHT. We had arrived!

THE
LEGENDARY
KING
SOLOMON

THE MOST CLEVER
MOUSE OF ALL

We found ourselves floating near a port, along a rocky coast. The Whisker Wafter had already TRANSFORMED to fit the time period — it was identical to the other ships we could see! No one would suspect that it was a sophisticated, modern time machine.

Robota used her tridimensional SCANNER to analyze the ships around us and compare them with the data in her electronic mega-brain. She buzzed for a few seconds, extracting the information. Then she said, "To your right are ancient Phoenician boats. To your left are boats from King Solomon's FLEET!"

"Cheesy creampuffs, we did it!" I squeaked for joy. "We finally made it!"

But Robota immediately continued, "Dear little cheesepuff, I wouldn't say that — technically we are in King Solomon's kingdom, but . . ."

"But . . ." I repeated, worried.

"Buut . . ." said Robota mysteriously.

"Buut . . . what?" I cried. "Tell me! My whiskers are wobbling from the stress!"

Robota patted my paw. "Who knows where we'll find the king? He could be anywhere. His kingdom is extremely large. Look!"

She **projected** a map of the kingdom, and my ears went limp with disappointment. It was enormouse! I began to tug desperately on my tail, shrieking, "Rancid ricotta, we'll never find him!"

Luckily, Thea hadn't lost hope. "We can't get DISCOURAGED now! We've come this far, so let's shake a tail. Everyone get dressed, and we'll start looking for the king. I'm sure we'll be able to get some **information** in the port."

THE KINGDOM OF KING SOLOMON
(AROUND 960 BCE)

Euphrates River

Palmyra

Damascus

Mediterranean Sea

Sea of Galilee

Jordan River

Jerusalem

Dead Sea

Petra

Ezion-Geber

Red Sea

THE KINGDOM OF KING SOLOMON

Solomon was the third king of the kingdom of Israel and is often remembered for his wisdom and ability to govern. Under his guidance (between about 970 BCE and 931 BCE), the kingdom of Israel prospered. Solomon organized the state in an efficient way, constructing numerous public buildings, developing commercial traffic, and establishing an important port on the Red Sea.

FASHION
IN THE AGE OF KING SOLOMON

Written accounts about clothing styles in the time of King Solomon aren't available, but we might imagine that the clothes were similar to those in the areas surrounding his kingdom.

HOW DO I PUT THIS ON?

Theat

Geronimot

CLOTHES FOR EVERY CLIMATE

Men and women probably wore long linen tunics beneath wool tunics. This way, they could tolerate the heat of the day but were also prepared for the cold of the night!

HEADDRESSES

The women may have worn a wrap on their heads to shade them from the sun. The men may have used a head covering similar to a turban, knotted on their heads.

As soon as we were ready, we left the Whisker Wafter and **SPLIT UP**, trying to figure out where King Solomon might be. We met up three hours later, but I was enormousely DISAPPOINTED: I hadn't discovered anything!

Bugsy Wugsy returned with a coral necklace, exclaiming, "Do you like it? A kind rodent **gave** it to me!"

Thea squeaked up. "I didn't find out anything

I didn't discover anything!

Rats!

I have mouserific news!

specific, but I did notice some movement at the ℗₀ℝ𝔱. There are guards everywhere!"

Just then, Benjamin ran to meet us, calling 𝖊𝖝𝖈𝖎𝖙𝖊𝖉𝖑𝖞, "I have mouserific news! There is a **very important mouse** arriving any minute now. I didn't find out where the king is, though."

The last to arrive, whistling and singing, was my cousin Trap. "Falala, falala, the most clever mouse of all! Falala, falala!"

Falala, falala!

WE'RE GOING TO
TRAVEL IN STYLE!

Cheese and crackers, we didn't have time for Trap's **shenanigans**! I asked, "Did you find anything out?"

Trap announced importantly, "Yes, of course! I figured out how to get comfortably to King Solomon's palace! I found a ride in the caravan of a noblemouse on her way to meet him!"

At that point, Robota (camouflaged as a brooch on my head covering), who had dozed off, suddenly woke up and **YELLED**, "Lets hurry along. We have to get to the king!"

I could hardly believe my ears. "**Marvemouse** job, Trap — we're going to travel in style! But exactly how will we be going? By horse? On the back of a donkey? In a sedan chair?"

Trap tugged on my right ear. "Cousin, you cheesebrain! **I** will travel in style in a sedan chair, since I am a scholar of the miraculous effects of essences. **You** will trek along as official porters of the treasure!"

Were my ears filled with cheese? "You're saying **the rest of us** will trek on paw?"

Trap gave my left ear a tug this time. "Quit your whining! What a fuss about a **LiTTLE WALK** in the desert!"

"A little walk!" I squeaked. I really had my tail in a twist now! "The desert **SuN** will fry our fur and roast our paws! Who knows how many days we'll have to walk, or how much the treasure will weigh!"

Trap held up a sack of **PRECiOUS STONES**. "You don't have a choice — I already signed you up and collected your salaries! I'll hang on to them, just to be safe. But stay calm! **Food** and

LODGING are free — though who knows what they'll give us to eat, and you'll have to sleep with the horses. I'm always thinking of you. Aren't you grateful?"

I wanted to **protest**, but Thea held up a paw. "We have to do it. At least we have a way to get to King Solomon's court!"

At **dawn** the next day, we went to where the caravan was getting ready to depart. There

were countless carts transporting sandalwood and precious stones, a cheeseload of camels carrying gold and spices, and tons of porters (like me!) carrying other gifts for King Solomon. Many soldiers guarded the caravan, since it was filled with enormouse riches.

For a **thousand** balls of mozzarella, what a squeaktacular spectacle!

When the caravan moved forward, Thea,

Benjamin, and Bugsy Wugsy secured a place on a **CART**, thanks to the handmaid that Bugsy Wugsy had made friends with the day before. I took a spot among the porters. Trap was relaxing on a fabumouse **sedan chair** and nibbling **figs** while two rodents walked next to him, waving large fans to keep him cool. Holey cheese, how annoying!

When I passed him, he said, "Cousin, as you can

Yum! Yum!

see, I don't need the *fascinating essence*. I'm a fascinating rodent all on my own!"

Rat-munching rattlesnakes, I didn't even have the strength to protest. After hours and hours of walking, I began to **stumble**, then crawl, and finally — I **FAINTED**!

Some mice threw me over the back of a horse and transported me like a sack of rotten figs roasting in the sun.

Rancid ricotta, what a terrible trip!

THE TEN DEGREES OF ROASTING GERONIMOT

1 For the first hour, everything was going fine.

2 In the second hour, my paws began to hurt and the blazing sun made my head pound.

3 In the third hour, I had blisters on my paws and my head was burning up!

4 In the fourth hour, my paws smoked and my brain boiled!

In the fifth hour, I couldn't feel my paws anymore and my head felt like gooey grilled cheese!

In the sixth hour, I was completely cooked and was starting to feel delirious.

In the seventh hour, I could barely stand.

In the eighth hour, I began to crawl.

In the ninth hour, I had a nervous breakdown and refused to go on.

Finally, some mice threw me over the back of a horse!

FINALLY AWAKE!

I recovered after many days under a spacious tent. When I finally woke up, I was lying on a soft **CARPET**, covered by a light wool blanket.

I shivered as the dawn breeze wafted by my burned snout. Next to me, Thea, Bugsy Wugsy, and Benjamin were sleeping deeply. My sister was clutching a linen cloth in her paw and had a basin of fresh **WATER** next to her. She had been using it to **COOL** my face! I was so thankful for my family — they had been taking care of me for who knows how long!

I got to my paws, head spinning, and wrapped myself in a blanket. In the **desert**, it's pretty chilly at night, though a mouse could easily die of heat during the day!

I peeked outside the tent and admired dawn in

the desert. What a sight! In the distance, I could see the city, white and shining in the early light of dawn. **How marvemouse!**

A tear rolled down my snout. It had been a very long, very tiring, and very, very, very dangerous journey. But soon we would be heading home, taking King Solomon's **ring** with us!

Thea, Bugsy Wugsy, and Benjamin woke up and threw their paws around me happily.

"How are you, big brother?" Thea asked, while Benjamin held me tightly and Bugsy Wugsy squeaked, "**Uncle G! I'm so happy!**"

I'll admit it — for once, I even enjoyed Bugsy Wugsy's squeaks!

Robota, who had gone back to her normal size and was standing by on low power mode, reactivated and raced over to me. "My cheesepuff! I was so **worried**! I was afraid I would become a widow before even officially becoming your fiancée! How tragic — it makes me want to **cry** just thinking about it!"

She began to sniffle, spraying tears everywhere. Oh, for the love of cheese!

Robota only calmed down once I promised her that, when we returned to New Mouse City, I would **INVITE** her out to dinner.

Suddenly, Trap entered the tent and **exclaimed**, "You're finally awake, Cousin! It's about time! Thank goodness I've gotten us

this far. I've been pretty fabumousc, right? At least one of us wasn't FRYING his brain with some death-defying stunts!"

I held up my paws. "It's not my fault that I roasted under the desert sun while you **relaxed** in a sedan chair!"

Trap just grinned and began to sing, "Ohhhh, Geronimo, Geronimo, he fried his little brain!"

Thea interrupted. "Enough FIGHTING, you two! We need to get to King Solomon's palace. This is the perfect moment for us to squeak with him and ask to borrow his **ring**!"

My sister was right! Without a moment to waste, we climbed onto some HORSes and trotted over to the palace. Robota shrunk down to a brooch again and returned to her spot on my head covering.

When we entered the palace, the noblemouse we had been traveling with had just finished offering the king some gifts. Solomon held her paw and said, "Noblemouse, of all the wonderful *jewels* that I've seen today, you are the most precious! Tell me, why have you come so far to see me?"

KING SOLOMON

She responded, "I wanted to know if your wisdom was as great as they say . . ."

The king smiled. "Good! Then I invite you to sit in on the hearings that are about to begin, so you can judge for yourself."

KING SOLOMON'S LEGENDARY RING

The king spent the morning squeaking with anyone who needed his **ADVICE**. Male and female rodents of all ages lined up to see him. Each of them had a **QUESTION** or a problem to resolve. Solomon listened to each mouse with great patience and offered up his infinite wisdom.

While we waited for our turn, Trap *nudged* me in the side and pointed at the sparkling ring on the king's paw. "Hey, Cousin, is that the famouse ring? Look, look, look — what a **huge emerald**!"

I craned my neck and peered at the ring. It appeared to be made of **solid gold** and adorned with an enormouse deep-green emerald.

It really was a fabumouse ring! But we hadn't

traveled through time, RISKING OUR TAILS, to find the ring because it was beautiful or valuable.

"Trap, you know we didn't come here because of the ring's value," I said quietly. "Legend says that it has the power to give wisdom and to bring harmony to nature."

"That's just what we need on our island," Benjamin squeaked up.

The line continued moving forward. Soon it would be our turn to speak with the king! Our mission was almost complete!

I couldn't help worrying. "Do you think the king will really trust us with such a precious, powerful object? After all, he knows nothing about us!"

I was so lost in my thoughts that I didn't realize it was our turn! SQUEAK!

Trap gave me a nudge in the right side,

Come on, it's our turn!

whispering, "Come on, you cheddarhead, it's our turn! Try not to embarrass us!"

Thea gave me a nudge in the left side. "Go, go, go — it's our turn!"

It's our turn!

Argh!

Robota gave me an electric shock to the whiskers, whispering, "Wake up, cheesepuff! You can do it!"

Oh, MOLDY mozzarella — the tremendmouse shock made me bolt forward!

I landed directly in front of the king's throne, paws shaking and whiskers wobbling. I immediately bowed so

Squeak!

deeply that my whiskers touched the ground, and waited for *King Solomon* to squeak to me.

After what seemed like forever, King Solomon looked me intensely in the eyes and said, "Mouse, you are not one of my **subjects**! Where do you come from, and why do you want to squeak with me?"

I nodded, hoping he couldn't see that even my fur was quivering. "Your Majesty, it's true, I am not one of your subjects. I come from an island very far away in **time** and SPACE. I'm sure that you have never heard of us, but we know all about your enormouse wisdom. I stand here in front of you as an *ambassador* of Mouse Island, asking for your help!"

The king smiled. "My good mouse, I will certainly help you if I can! *What would you ask of me?*"

I felt **drops** of sweat slide

down my whiskers. This was it! I had to ask to borrow the **PING**.

But how would the king **REACT**?

I cleared my throat. "Your Majesty, the rodents on our island have lost balance and harmony. The **water** and the **air** are polluted, and all the animals are suffering. For this reason . . . well . . . I . . . I would like . . . but I'm not sure if . . ."

"Mouse, tell me what you need before I lose my **patience**!" the king squeaked gruffly.

I gathered my **COURAGE** and asked everything in one breath.

"Doyouthinkyoucouldloanme yourpreciouslegendaryringIwould bringitrightbackmouse'shonor!"

Huh?

Oops!

Then I fell silent, **waiting** for the king's reaction.

A strange expression crossed his snout, and he began to Fiddle with his beard.

I couldn't stand the suspense. *Thundering cattails!*

What if he got **mad**?

What if he refUSEd to loan us the ring?

The king's paws played with the tufts of his **BEARD**, and his expression became even stranger. After a silence that seemed to go on forever, the corners of

Hmmm . . .

Thundering cattails!

his **mouth** turned up and suddenly . . .

The king burst into laughter!

Holey cheese, what was going on?

"Hee, hee, hee, ha, ha, ha, ho, ho, ho, ho, ho, ho, ho, ho, ho! Oh, what a funny mouse you are! But I'm afraid there is a TERRIBLE misconception. Follow me, and I will explain the secret of the ring!"

HO HO HO HO HO HO HO HO HO HO HO HO HO

THE SECRET
OF THE RING

By now it was twilight. The king got to his paws, offered his arm to the noblemouse, and motioned for us to follow him into his GARDEN.

It was a marvemouse place — everything seemed to be in perfect harmony. The stems of the flourishing PLANTS lushly stretched toward the sky, which glowed a pure and brilliant blue. The birds sang a beautiful evening song, and the *flowers* gave off a fabumouse scent.

King Solomon asked us to sit on a group of stone benches, which were set in a **circle** to form a ring of stone. Once everyone was comfortable, he smiled. "I love this place! This is where I meet with my most loyal advisors, because when we are sitting in this **circle**, no one is more important than anyone else." He grabbed a stick and drew a circle on the ground. "I will reveal a secret: the golden ring that I wear is only a jewel and nothing more — it has no powers! The only thing that creates balance and harmony in nature is **love** and **RESPECT** among all creatures. Everyone plays a role. In that circle, every living species of plants and animals has equal **IMPORTANCE**."

He paused, looking each of us in the eyes. Then he held up his ring.

"The true ring of wisdom is not this one with the large emerald. No, it's the **STONE RiNG**, where we are sitting now. If you want to bring harmony and balance to your faraway island, you don't need my jewel. You all just need to meet and decide on a plan, all together. This is the only way you can truly resolve your **problems**!"

He added, "Remember that every mouse

must do his or her part to bring *balance* and *harmony* to your island!"

We were all silent, thinking hard about the wise words we had just heard.

The noblemouse looked sweetly at King Solomon. "My king, you really are as wise as they say!"

He responded with a *smile*. "And you are the most beautiful mouse I have ever seen!"

Robota sighed and whispered to me, "Oh, how romantic! He knows how to say nice things to his beloved. Unlike you — you never compliment me!"

I whispered, "Well, that's because you are **NOT** my beloved! And I am **NOT** your beloved. Don't get any cheesebrained ideas!"

But Robota was one persistent robot. "I'll figure out how to change your mind, **MOUSE** of my heart! Don't forget, you invited me out for **dinner**!"

I begged her to be quiet. That robot sure knew how to ruin a solemn moment!

After a minute, I got to my paws and said, "Thank you, Your Majesty, for your wise advice. Now we ask your permission to return home. We will tell everyone what we learned about the secret of the ring!"

Thank you, Your Majesty, for your wise advice!

WE'RE GOING HOME!

King Solomon gave us three very fast horses to take us across the **desert**, back to the Whisker Wafter.

We thanked him and left immediately. Holey cheese, I was so happy not to be stumbling on my paws through the desert this time! We *galloped* under the stars in the cold night. I felt so small under that enormouse sky! It

almost looked like it was studded with diamonds.

We **galloped** into the golden light of dawn, and then under the hot noon sun. We **galloped** on and on, until the sun went down again, and for another whole night and day.

Cheese niblets — I was so rattled from all that galloping that I couldn't feel my tail, and it felt like my brain was bouncing around in my head!

While I clung to my saddle, King Solomon's words echoed in my mind: "Balance . . . harmony . . . love . . . respect."

I tried to figure out how to use the king's advice to **SAVE** the environment on Mouse Island, but my poor brain was all mixed up like a mozzarella milkshake! I muttered to myself, "We need a seriously **MOUSERIFIC IDEA** . . ."

I have an idea!

Luckily, Benjamin (who was riding along with me on my horse) heard me. "Uncle G, why don't we just do what the king said? We can organize a conference of all the rodents on Mouse Island to decide how to save the environment!"

Bugsy Wugsy squeaked, "**All** the rodents? But there are too many of us!"

Trap added, "We would need an **ENORMOUSE** room, with an **ENORMOUSE** table and an **ENORMOUSE** buffet . . ." He trailed off for a minute, rubbing his belly. "**Yum!** On the other paw, maybe we could just do the enormouse buffet!"

"We could gather the **representatives** from all the cities on Mouse Island, along with scientists and environmental experts," Thea suggested.

I felt like squeaking for joy. "What a mouserific idea!"

After that, our excitement helped the time to pass very quickly. Before we knew it, we were on the Whisker Watter. To my dismay, Trap reached the computer first . . . but this time, he chose the right cube! **WHEW!**

We felt the usual vibration, then a FLASH OF WHITE LIGHT, and we were navigating on the Ocean of Infinite Time for the last time.

"We're going hooooooooome!" I cried.

WELCOME HOME!

Everyone squeaked **happily** — we had completed our mission! Bugsy Wugsy, Benjamin, and Robota took me by the paws, and we all began to **JUMP** with happiness.

Cheese and crackers — I definitely should have avoided those jumps! The **whisker wafter** had already started to sway and sway . . .

This time, my fur turned an awful shade of green. Oh, I was going to toss my cheese!

To make matters worse, Robota started talking my ear off again. "My little cheesepuff, have you decided where to take me to dinner yet? You should choose a romantic spot . . .

"I imagine a candlelit dinner with violins serenading us," Robota went on. "The atmosphere has to be just right when you give me

Cheesepuff, are you taking me to dinner?

Rancid ricotta!

the **engagement** ring, understand? Speaking of which, have you decided on a ring? I would like a nice DIAMOND or a **SAPPHIRE** or an **emerald** — or maybe all three!"

I tried **AGAIN** to explain that she was a really nice robot, but I didn't plan to get engaged . . . and she was extremely **offended**. But rather than not speaking to me, Robota decided to torture me by summarizing her plans for the **wedding**! Rancid ricotta, I couldn't win!

Luckily, Benjamin and Bugsy Wugsy came to the rescue. Bugsy Wugsy cut in, squeaking, "Uncle G, what do you say we get to work immediately, implementing King Solomon's advice? We could write a book full of ways to save nature and the environment!"

Benjamin added, "We can distribute it during the conference we're going to organize."

What a fabumouse **idea**! After we put on our normal clothes, we met in the Whisker Wafter's library to work on the **BOOK**.

Getting down to work actually helped take my mind off my stomachache!

Bugsy Wugsy and Benjamin had a cheeseload of marvemouse ideas. Robota offered to take notes, but then started rambling on and on and on. "Cheesepuff, since I'm performing an essential service for the book (after all, if I weren't here, you would not be able to type a single word!), **my name** must be on the cover! Nice and big!"

I threw my paws in the air and agreed. What else could I do? I just wanted to get back to

working on our enormousely important book!

While I dictated the text of the book, Robota continued to COMPLAIN. "Cheesepuff, speak slower! How do you spell *pollution*? With a *T* or an *S*? Ecology is written with a *K*?"

"Great balls of mozzarella, for a robot, you are not very good at SPELLING!" I squeaked, ready to tear out my whiskers. "Shouldn't you be an expert?"

Do you spell that with a C?

"It's not my fault!" Robota protested. "It's a small defect in production. The dictation program doesn't work well, and Professor von Volt hasn't installed the spell checker yet!"

Anyway, with a **CHEESELOAD** of patience and the help of Benjamin and Bugsy Wugsy, we were able to write the whole book during our journey. Holey cheese! We had just finished when a *FLASH OF WHITE LIGHT* let us know that we had arrived — we were home again!

As we left the deck of the Whisker Wafter, we found ourselves inside a **metal** dome. On a platform nearby, we could see Professor von Volt, Dewey von Volt, Margo Bitmouse, Rusty Carr, and all the other members of the von Volt family, waiting for us!

PASSWORD: SAVE NATURE!

We hugged our friends, then boarded the *Incredible Airship*, which would bring us back to New Mouse City. Professor von Volt offered us a mousetastic **buffet**. There were cream puffs with Parmesan shavings, cheese tarts with hazelnuts, mini ricotta and strawberry soufflés, and mozzarella-vanilla MILKSHAKES. Yum!

Slurp!

How tasty!

Yum!

Once we had recovered from our journey, Professor von Volt invited us to follow him to the conference room of the Incredible Airship, where the entire von Volt family joined us again.

The professor seated us around a large crystal table. "Geronimo, were you able to get to the age of *King Solomon?* Did you squeak with him? Did he give you the famous ring that brings harmony and balance to the environment?"

I smiled. "My dear friend, we don't have the ring — as it turns out, nothing like that exists! The ring of King Solomon is not actually a jewel, but a group of **STONE BENCHES** placed in a circle, where he and his advisors have discussions in order to make wise decisions."

Everyone murmured in **DISAPPOINTMENT**, "Oh no! Now what will we do?"

Thea said, "We don't have the ring, but we do have the precious *advice* of the wise king! He suggested that we have a meeting to resolve our problems. Every single one of us needs to do our part to bring harmony and balance back to the environment."

I added, "We were thinking about organizing a large conference, including all the scientists, environmental experts, and mayors of MOUSE ISLAND. Together, we can decide on a strategy to protect the ENVIRONMENT!"

I paused and looked each of the von Volt family members in the eyes. "What do you think — are you in? Will you help us organize a super-enormouse-mega-conference to save Mouse Island's environment?"

Everyone leaped to their paws and exclaimed, "Count me in! What a mouserific idea!"

I smiled. "Now that everyone is on board, there's a lot to do. Let's get our tails in gear!"

We got to work immediately!

PASSWORD: SAVE NATURE!

Margo Bitmouse designed a beautiful website to publicize the conference, entitled: "The Ring of Wisdom: How to Save Mouse Island's Environment!"

Thea helped write the text for the site and contacted all the environmental experts on Mouse Island.

Rusty Carr and Roborat 8 worked on coming up with plans for nonpolluting modes of transportation.

Dewey and Vivian von Volt studied different ways to produce clean energy.

Benjamin and Bugsy Wugsy kept tremendmousely busy by calling the mayors from the different cities around Mouse Island to invite them to the conference.

And Trap was busy, too . . . finishing all the leftover tarts from the buffet! Then he took a nap, **$norinɡ** like a steamroller.

When I woke him up, he swatted at me with his paws. "Aw, come on, Gerrykins! You said that each one of us should do what we're best at — and I'm best at **EATING** and **Nɑppinɡ**. Everyone knows that!"

I rolled my eyes. "You actually have another specialty: **COOKING**! Why don't you organize the meals for the conference?"

Trap leaped to his paws, put on an apron and

Mmmmmm, delicious!

chef's **HAT**, and exclaimed, "I'm the best cook in New Mouse City — this is the perfect job for me! For once, cheddarhead, you're **right**!"

While he got to work, I began to revise and edit the book that I had written with Benjamin, Bugsy Wugsy, and Robota. We had decided to leave space to add new chapters during the conference, with **suggestions** from all the scientists and environmental experts about what each rodent could do to protect the environment. But I wanted the part that was already written to be pawsitively PERFECT!

Correct this!

Everyone was busy working when the **INCREDIBLE** Airship

anchored on the roof of *The Rodent's Gazette*. We hurried into the newsroom, where GRANDFATHER WILLIAM welcomed us.

"I'm happy to see you, Grandson!" he boomed. "It's about time you got back here! While you were off having fun and *relaxing*, we worked our paws off. So roll up your sleeves and get back to work!"

I tried to SMILE — rat-munching rattlesnakes, my time away had been anything but fun and relaxing! My grandfather squeaks things like this all the time, but I know he cares about me. So I hugged him and said, "I'm HAPPY to see you, too! Thanks for taking care of things while I was away."

I'll take charge!

I filled everyone in on our marvemouse *journey* and told them all about the conference we wanted to organize.

Grandfather looked impressed. *"Fabumouse job, Grandson.* This is what I'm squeaking about! To show my support, I'll take charge. I am the cat's meow when it comes to being in charge — as **overworked** as I am, I never overwork others. Don't worry. I'll get everyone's whiskers in line!"

I wanted to tell him that he had been overworking me for years, but I didn't have a chance. He had already gathered the whole staff of *The Rodent's Gazette* and put them to work before I could even squeak! Holey cheese!

Seven Days Later . . .

Seven days later, everything was ready! An enormouse cheese-colored tent went up in the park of New Mouse City, complete with everything necessary to host the **mega-conference**! There was a truly gigantic meeting table in the shape of a ring, a LABORATORY for scientific analysis, a pressroom, a **buffet** (organized by Trap, of course!), a break room, a barber for arranging *whiskers* after many hours of work, and even a **GYM** with a masseuse for putting crooked necks and tails back

in line after sitting at the computer for too long!

On the first official day of the conference, all the **MAYORS** of Mouse Island arrived. There were representatives from Frozen Fur Peak to the Mouschara Desert, from Swissville to San Mouscisco, from Ratzikistan to the Rattytrap Jungle. They were joined by all the SCIENTISTS and environmental experts: geologists, biologists, meteorologists, entomologists, volcanologists, speleologists, ethologists, rattologists . . . cheese and crackers! All the best brains of Mouse Island were meeting around a **table**, just as King Solomon had suggested!

Thanks!

Take this, it's for you!

Next!

Everyone squeaked up with their different ideas about how to save and protect the environment.

After seven days of speeches and discussions, an **emergency plan** was unanimously approved. At the end of the seventh day I was a mousely mess, but I was also happy and tremendmousely proud of what we'd done.

I said good-bye to my FRiENDS one by one. The last to leave was Professor von Volt, who shook my paw and said,

"THANKS, GERONIMO! Because of you, I think we'll actually be able to save Mouse Island!"

Thanks, Geronimo!

I shook my snout. "Oh, no, professor, I just did my part like everyone else! Really, thank you — without you, we never would have been able to travel through time and meet the wise King Solomon."

As Professor von Volt waved good-bye, I turned to head into the office to finish my book . . . when Robota suddenly jumped out of nowhere! "So, sweetwhiskers, did you forget about our romantic dinner? And you weren't planning to finish writing the book without me, right? Remember that my name is going to be on the cover, **nice and big**!"

Great balls of mozzarella, I couldn't forget that if I tried! So, that night, I invited Robota

Oh, for the love of cheese!

Sweetwhiskers!

to **dinner**. Putrid Parmesan, she tormented me all night by chattering about her wedding plans! Finally, I explained to her that we should just be friends, and she agreed!

Over the next few days, I worked with Robota day in and day out to finish the book.

Thankfully, in the end, the **BOOK** turned out to be fabumouse! It's full of useful information, including many small and simple things that each one of us can do to save and protect the environment. If everyone works together, we can make this world a better place! I had to travel through time to figure that out, but I'm honored to pass that wisdom along to my readers — or my name isn't *Stilton, Geronimo Stilton*!

Join me and my friends as we travel through time in these very special editions!

THE JOURNEY THROUGH TIME

BACK IN TIME:
THE SECOND JOURNEY THROUGH TIME

THE RACE AGAINST TIME:
THE THIRD JOURNEY THROUGH TIME

LOST IN TIME:
THE FOURTH JOURNEY THROUGH TIME

NO TIME TO LOSE:
THE FIFTH JOURNEY THROUGH TIME

Be sure to read all my fabumouse adventures!

#1 Lost Treasure of the Emerald Eye

#2 The Curse of the Cheese Pyramid

#3 Cat and Mouse in a Haunted House

#4 I'm Too Fond of My Fur!

#5 Four Mice Deep in the Jungle

#6 Paws Off, Cheddarface!

#7 Red Pizzas for a Blue Count

#8 Attack of the Bandit Cats

#9 A Fabumouse Vacation for Geronimo

#10 All Because of a Cup of Coffee

#11 It's Halloween, You 'Fraidy Mouse!

#12 Merry Christmas, Geronimo!

#13 The Phantom of the Subway

#14 The Temple of the Ruby of Fire

#15 The Mona Mousa Code

#16 A Cheese-Colored Camper

#17 Watch Your Whiskers, Stilton!

#18 Shipwreck on the Pirate Islands

#19 My Name Is Stilton, Geronimo Stilton

#20 Surf's Up, Geronimo!

#21 The Wild, Wild West

#22 The Secret of Cacklefur Castle

A Christmas Tale

#23 Valentine's Day
Disaster

#24 Field Trip to
Niagara Falls

#25 The Search for
Sunken Treasure

#26 The Mummy
with No Name

#27 The Christmas
Toy Factory

#28 Wedding
Crasher

#29 Down and Out
Down Under

#30 The Mouse Island
Marathon

#31 The Mysterious
Cheese Thief

Christmas Catastrophe

#32 Valley of the
Giant Skeletons

#33 Geronimo and the
Gold Medal Mystery

#34 Geronimo Stilton,
Secret Agent

#35 A Very Merry
Christmas

#36 Geronimo's
Valentine

#37 The Race Across
America

#38 A Fabumouse
School Adventure

#39 Singing Sensation

#40 The Karate Mouse

#41 Mighty Mount
Kilimanjaro

#42 The Peculiar
Pumpkin Thief

#43 I'm Not a
Supermouse!

#44 The Giant
Diamond Robbery

#45 Save the White
Whale!

#46 The Haunted
Castle

#47 Run for the Hills, Geronimo!

#48 The Mystery in Venice

#49 The Way of the Samurai

#50 This Hotel Is Haunted!

#51 The Enormouse Pearl Heist

#52 Mouse in Space!

#53 Rumble in the Jungle

#54 Get into Gear, Stilton!

#55 The Golden Statue Plot

#56 Flight of the Red Bandit

#57 The Stinky Cheese Vacation

#58 The Super Chef Contest

#59 Welcome to Moldy Manor

#60 The Treasure of Easter Island

#61 Mouse House Hunter

#62 Mouse Overboard!

#63 The Cheese Experiment

#64 Magical Mission

#65 Bollywood Burglary

#66 Operation: Secret Recipe

#67 The Chocolate Chase

#68 Cyber-Thief Showdown

#69 Hug a Tree, Geronimo

Up Next!